I0608032

Grave Mistake

HEDGEWITCH FOR HIRE - BOOK 1

CHRISTINE POPE

This is a work of fiction. Names, characters, places, and incidents are either the product of the author's imagination or are used fictitiously. Any resemblance to actual events, places, organizations, or persons, whether living or dead, is entirely coincidental.

GRAVE MISTAKE

Copyright © 2021 by Christine Pope

ISBN: 978-1-946435-39-2

Published by Dark Valentine Press

Cover design by Lou Harper

Ebook formatting by Indie Author Services

All rights reserved. No part of this book may be reproduced in any form or by any electronic or mechanical means, including information storage and retrieval systems—except in the case of brief quotations embodied in critical articles or reviews—without permission in writing from its publisher, Dark Valentine Press.

The Pits and the Pendulum

MAZEY HOSKINS, THE OWNER OF CRESCENT City—my favorite witchy supply shop—leaned over the counter as I began to pull out my debit Visa card and said in a conspiratorial murmur, "Word on the street is that Lucien Dumond is coming for you."

Although I generally did my best to maintain a Zen attitude, no matter what troubles might cross my path, her words still sent a sharp stab of worry through me. But I managed to smile, even as I tried to tell myself that Mazey was probably exaggerating things. I loved Mazey—she was like the cozy, friendly grandmother I'd never had—but boy, did she love to trade stories.

Most of the time, I did, too, since chatting with Mazey was one of the best ways to stay in touch with what might be happening in the various local magical groups. Even in this connected age, rumors tended to stay off the internet when it came to L.A's pagan community. The last thing any of us wanted was to give some ammo to the mundanes…aka, those who didn't believe in magic of any sort.

However, the tale she'd just related was one I definitely didn't want to hear. Several practitioners who'd come down on Lucien Dumond's bad side had disappeared from the scene. The rumor was that they'd simply decided to relocate, but darker whispers hinted that Lucien might have come up with a more permanent solution to his problems.

Doing my best to shrug off Mazey's comment, I said lightly, "He's probably pissed off that I turned him down for another date," then handed over my debit card. "Guy can't take no for an answer."

Which was definitely not an exaggeration. Lucien Dumond was the leader of GLANG—the Greater Los Angeles Necromancers' Guild—and he attracted groupies like the Rolling Stones on a worldwide tour back in the '60s. Not that I'd been around to witness those sorts of shenanigans, of course, but still, I'd read a few stories.

Despite Lucien already having a slavishly devoted group of women—whom I tended to refer to as his harem—he was always on the prowl for fresh meat. Unfortunately, a while back, he'd decided I was exactly the kind of meat he wanted.

Mazey shook her head. "Selena, I don't think this is something you should ignore. People are saying that he wants to shut you down…by whatever means necessary."

Again, I had to fight back a wave of unease. I'd been hearing a whisper of rumors along those lines for a few weeks already, but this was the first time anyone had come right out and told me to my face that I might be in actual danger, that Lucien might have decided it was time to get rid of the troublesome pebble in his shoe.

Trust Mazey to do the hard work. Since she wasn't really a practitioner, except to amuse herself, she hadn't crossed the leader of GLANG and his band of lackeys.

I, on the other hand, was a "hedgewitch," a phrase used to describe a practitioner who worked on her own, who had her own way of approaching the arcane arts. My psychic abilities had come on early, and I'd basically trained myself, first from books I got at the library and ordered online, then later on by watching YouTube videos to help fill in the gaps. I didn't follow any particular practice, but picked and chose from a variety of different disciplines as they suited my own particular talents. Most people tended to think I was a practicing Wiccan, but I really wasn't, although I called out to certain Celtic deities, such as Cerridwen and Brigid, as the need arose.

At any rate, I was basically the antithesis of Lucien Dumond and his squad. He'd trained with a master on the East Coast, and he pretty strictly followed the rulebook of the Order of the Golden Dawn, a secret society that was the predecessor to Wicca...although with his own unique twist.

Anyway, Lucien had been trying to coax me to his way of doing things—and into his bed—for the last year or so. Before then, I probably had barely been a blip on his radar, since he hadn't seen me as any kind of a threat. But then I got a client who ended up following my advice and landed a starring role in a hot new TV series, and suddenly Lucien realized there was another skilled practitioner in the L.A. area, one who quite possibly had poached a client who should have gone to him.

"Last I checked, this was a free country," I said, and watched as Mazey, expression still troubled, slipped my debit card into the chip reader before handing it back. "I mean, even Lucien can't think he's entitled to every new client in L.A."

"No, only the ones who can bring him a lot of money," she responded pithily. Her expression had turned resigned, as if she'd guessed that I wasn't going to heed her warnings and was now trying to tell herself that she'd done her best and could wash her hands of the whole affair.

I shrugged. Performing readings for people over the past ten years had allowed me to develop something of a poker face, so I hoped she couldn't pick up anything of the worry that had begun to churn in my gut. It was easy to be dismissive in order to let her think the whole situation was no big deal, but I knew better...even if I didn't know what I should do next.

Tone dry, I said, "I doubt Lucien Dumond is hurting for cash," and Mazey let out an unwilling chuckle.

"No, probably not."

I picked up my bag of herbs, stuffed it in my purse—I had several candles I wanted to pour for my new moon observance—and thanked her, then hurried out of the shop. A little ways down the street, my Denim Edition Volkswagen Beetle awaited. I got behind the wheel and pulled away from the curb.

The thought crossed my mind that maybe I should have picked a slightly less conspicuous car a few years back when I'd finally decided to replace my ancient Nissan Sentra, but then I wanted to shake my head at myself. Yes, GLANG was nothing to trifle with, but even that group of sorcerers and witches didn't number more than thirty or forty people at the most. It wasn't as if Lucien could have spies planted on every street corner in L.A., or operatives capable of hacking into L.A.'s traffic-cam system.

At least, I didn't think he did.

Frowning, I headed for home, which was a rent-controlled duplex I'd been lucky enough to find more than five years earlier. Or really, it probably wasn't luck so much as a home-manifestation spell that had turned out exactly the way I wanted.

I parked in the carport, waved to my neighbor —Mr. Hanley, a retired aerospace engineer—then went inside. At once, the comforting scent of sage and incense surrounded me, and I let out a breath. In my house, with its shabby chic collection of mismatched furniture and my carefully curated collection of crystals and art, I felt safe.

Too bad that just because it felt that way, it didn't mean it actually was.

After putting my bag of herbs and my purse down on the little round table in the dining area, I stood in my living room, irresolute. Mazey's words worried me more than I'd let on. Yes, I'd been doing this dance around Lucien, trying my hardest to pretend I had no idea what he wanted from me, but clearly, he was tired of doing the avoidance two-step and was ready to play hardball.

If you'll pardon the mixed metaphors.

I went into the kitchen and put the kettle on, figuring a nice calming cup of tea might be just what I needed to settle my nerves. Yes, it was a glorious spring day, one of those perfect seventy-five-degree slices of heaven that you often got in Los Angeles in the springtime, but I still thought a hot drink would help.

Or maybe I just needed something to occupy myself.

My brain churned away, testing and then discarding various possibilities. That I would throw up my hands and meekly give in to Lucien Dumond was just not an option. Yes, the guy had a certain reptilian charisma, but it definitely wasn't anything I personally found attractive. And that didn't even take into account his "business model."

His group was called the "Greater Los Angeles Necromancers' Guild," but it wasn't as though he and his cohorts were going around Southern California and digging up bodies for reanimation spells. No, they used their powers for something much subtler. Instead, the enchantments they cast were put to use keeping people preternaturally youthful. You know those actors and actresses who barely seem to age, who keep working decade after decade with hardly any loss of vitality?

In one case out of ten, it was awesome genetics and some extremely good cosmetic surgery, and nothing more. In all the rest... GLANG had been on the job. I probably don't have to point out that there's a lot of money in that sort of work. Because there was a lot of money involved, Lucien wanted to make sure no one interfered with the magic he invoked to create that false youthfulness.

And no, the actress I'd helped land the perfect role wasn't anywhere close to the age where she'd be needing that sort of assistance, but Lucien was all about the long game. He wanted to have been her savior so he could start cultivating a relationship that would last decades. Maybe she didn't need anything smoothed or tightened right now...but in ten years or so, that would be an entirely different story.

Which was why he was so annoyed with me. As long as I dispensed advice to dissatisfied housewives and anxiety-ridden lawyers and dentists, he couldn't care less what I did. But as soon as I horned in on his territory—Hollywood—well, that was an entirely different situation.

Sigh.

I briefly considered going straight to him and promising I wouldn't take any more clients in the entertainment industry. That seemed like a cowardly thing to do, though. The guy wasn't some all-powerful god—he was just a sorcerer who'd actually been born Luke Dershowitz, the oldest son of a very successful oral surgeon in Encino. Why should I have to bow and scrape to him?

Because he's a lot more powerful than you are, I thought then, although that wasn't strictly the truth. He was really good at invoking some of the world's darker forces to firm an actress's jaw line or nudge a few pounds off some aging actor's waist, but his real power lay in the witches—male and female—he'd gathered around him. If nothing else, Lucien was very good at getting people to become followers, and when he combined his own powers with theirs, they constituted a force that a solitary witch didn't have a chance of beating.

That I'd refused to become one of his acolytes...on top of letting him know I had no interest in jumping in the sack with him...well, no wonder I was probably number one on what my mother referred to as a "fecal roster."

Another option would be to flat-out ignore Lucien. That proposition, of course, would be a hell of a lot riskier. He liked to stay in his fancy mid-century modern house in the hills above his hometown of Encino, but he ventured out from time to time if necessary...and putting down an impudent hedgewitch was probably reason enough to draw him down to West L.A. If nothing else, coming down hard on me would serve as an object lesson to anyone else who might have been contemplating getting in his way.

I briefly considered reaching out to some of the other witches I knew for help, but even if they agreed with my opinion of Lucien Dumond, none of them were strong enough to take on GLANG. Like me, they tried to fly low and avoid the radar.

Except I hadn't done such a great job of that, had I?

Double sigh.

The third option was one I really didn't want to consider. Since Lucien viewed Southern California as his territory, I could just...leave. Pull up stakes and go someplace where he couldn't be bothered to follow me, just like those other witches and warlocks who'd made the mistake of making an enemy of Lucien Dumond.

If they'd really left at all, and hadn't ended up buried in a shallow grave in the Angeles National Forest or something.

As soon as the thought of running away crossed my mind, I wanted to immediately reject it. Why the hell should I have to leave my treasured little duplex, my clients, the quiet life I'd built for myself? I didn't have a lot of relatives— my mother still lived in Sherman Oaks, where I'd grown up, although I didn't have any other imme-diate family—but L.A. was still my home. Why should I let someone like Lucien Dumond chase me out of my home?

Because he's a ruthless jackass, I told myself. *He doesn't think the regular standards of morality apply to him.*

Again, nothing more than the truth. Yes, he wanted to add me as another notch on his bedpost if possible, but at the same time, he prob-ably wouldn't scruple to fit me with the sorcerous equivalent of cement shoes and drop me off the Santa Monica Pier if I didn't toe the line he'd drawn in the sand.

Scowling, I measured some Darjeeling into a pierced aluminum ball and dropped it into a teapot, then poured hot water over it. Fragrant steam rose to my nostrils. Usually, I would have closed my eyes and breathed it in, allowing myself to enjoy the aroma, but I was in no mood right then.

I got out a cup and picked up the teapot, then took both items with me into the living room. Since an embroidered cloth from India covered part of the coffee table, I knew it was safe to set down the pot once I was done pouring myself a cup. However, I didn't drink right away. No, I went to fetch the one thing I generally turned to when I needed advice.

My favorite Tarot deck.

After slipping the cards out of the velvet bag where I stored them to ward off any stray vibrations, I held them in my hands for a moment, focusing on my intentions. Or rather, letting the universe know that I could definitely use a little guidance.

All right. Time to see what the universe had to say.

I pulled out a card and set it down on the coffee table a few inches away from my teacup.

Oh, great.

The Tower card stared up at me, lightning outlining the slender shape of the structure, illuminating the forms of the hapless people who'd thrown themselves off in a desperate attempt to save themselves.

Well, that was a message, all right…just not the one I'd been hoping to get.

That card signified upheaval, change, sudden transformations.

In other words, it seemed to me as though my hope for continuing a quiet life in my duplex wasn't, as they say, in the cards.

Annoyed, I scooped up the Tower and shuffled it back into the deck. After all, it wasn't as though enlightenment was always delivered on the first try. Sometimes I had to make several attempts before the meaning the cards were trying to impart really made any sense.

I pulled a card.

The Tower again.

Coincidence?

Probably not.

"All right," I said aloud. Sometimes I liked to talk to the universe that way, as if somewhere deep down, I thought it might hear me better if I spoke rather than merely thought. "Clearly, I need a change. What's your suggestion?"

Leaving the Tower card down where I'd placed it on the table, I waited for a few seconds, then withdrew another card from the deck.

The World.

Hmm. That card could mean completion, accomplishment…or it could mean travel. And if I really was going to turn tail and run, then I supposed relocation would include travel. But where?

I picked up the two cards and shuffled them back into the deck. And shuffled. And shuffled. I figured if the Tower came up again, then clearly it meant I was supposed to throw myself off one, since I didn't have many other options.

But I didn't pull the Tower. No, this time, my repeat card was The World.

"Okay," I told the universe. "I get it. You think I've completed my run here in L.A. and it's time to move on. Some help on exactly where would be useful."

Another shuffle, another card pull.

The World.

All right, this was getting ridiculous. Maybe it was time to try something else.

I took a few sips of tea, then got up from the sofa and went to the cabinet where I stored my pendulum and my divining cloth, which basically looked much like a Ouija board, with the alphabet printed on it, along with "yes" and "no" and the four cardinal directions as well. Both items in hand, I walked over to the dining room table and spread the cloth out on it, then waited for a moment, the fluorite pendulum clutched in one palm in order to pick up more of its vibrations.

"Where am I going?" I asked, then dangled the pendulum over the tabletop.

It swung idly back and forth, moving from the letter "A" to the letter "Z." And kept swinging, much longer than it should have. A to Z, Z to A.

Flummoxed, I could only stare at it. "Somewhere between A and Z?" I asked aloud. "Could you be a little more specific?"

It described one more arc between the A and the Z, and then moved, picking out a series of letters.

G-L-O-B-E.

The pendulum stopped then, hanging still above the printed mat I used for divinations.

Globe. Was that another way of saying "the World"? Was it referencing the Greater Arcana card I had pulled a few minutes earlier?

In which case, I'd come full circle and still hadn't learned a damn thing of any use.

For a few seconds, I stood there, the pendulum dangling from my hand. Should I try asking again?

Like that had done any good when I was pulling Tarot cards.

A sudden thought popped into my mind. On a shelf in the second bedroom, the one I'd turned into an office, sat the globe I'd used when I was in grade school. Why I'd hung onto it through all those years and multiple moves, I had no idea, but maybe the universe was telling me I needed to use the globe to find the place where I'd be traveling. The theory made just about as much sense as anything else.

I set the pendulum down on the tabletop, then hurried back to my office. Yes, there was the globe, pushed all the way into the back corner, nearly obscured by a file box. Going on my tiptoes, I reached up for the globe and wrapped my fingers around the base. It teetered precipitously as I pulled it toward me, and I had to grab for it with both hands to avoid getting smacked in the head as it slipped off the edge of the shelf.

Careful, I scolded myself, *or your next "journey" is going to be to the emergency room.*

But since I hadn't gotten hit on the head by the thing, I carried it over to the desk where my laptop sat. I pushed the computer out of the way to give myself more room, then set down the globe and regarded it warily for a moment. What happened next could decide my future. And yes, I knew that some people would think it was crazy to make huge, life-changing decisions based on a flip of a card or the swing of a pendulum...or a rotation of a child's globe...but I actually thought it was crazier to ignore such things. The universe was always sending us messages; the big problem was that most people tended to ignore those signals.

I pulled in a breath and then spun the globe lightly with my hand. The old kid's game—spin the globe and see where you're going to go. Only in this case, it really wasn't a game.

Still holding my breath, I placed the tip of my index finger against the globe's surface, feeling the little bumps and flat areas pass by. The globe spun, then slowed.

Came to a stop.

The breath escaped my lips as I leaned in

close, eyes taking in the familiar outlines of the place where my finger had landed.

Arizona.

A to Z.

I wanted to laugh. The pendulum had been as literal as it could be, and I still hadn't gotten its message.

Okay, Arizona. That wasn't so bad. No, I wasn't big on heat, but from what I could tell, the place where the globe had stopped wasn't in Phoenix. I narrowed my eyes, trying to figure out exactly where I was supposed to go. As far as I could tell, there wasn't anything in that particular spot, just mountains and desert.

What, was I supposed to go live like a hermit in a cave or something?

Obviously, a little more research would be required.

I picked up the globe and set it on the floor, then opened my laptop and logged in. My plan was to look at a map of Arizona online, something that would provide a lot more detail than the major cities called out on the toy globe's surface.

With a map displayed on my laptop's screen, I zoomed in on Phoenix and started moving slowly to the east and north, since that seemed to be roughly the direction where my finger had landed. Slowly…slowly….

And then I stopped, an unwilling laugh escaping my lips.

Talk about literal. Once again, I'd completely missed the point my pendulum was trying to get across.

Because there it was, staring up at me from the screen.

Globe, Arizona.

2

Online Shopping

I'd never heard of Globe, Arizona. A few minutes of research told me the reason why. It was a tiny place, just a little more than seven thousand people. Hell, my high school had been bigger than that.

What was I supposed to do in an isolated former mining town tucked away in the mountains east of Phoenix?

Hide, of course. It did seem like just about the last place where Lucien Dumond would think to look for me.

I did a quick image search on Globe, just to know what I was getting into, and what I found relieved some of my anxiety. Sure, the town was small, but the downtown area looked very cute, like something out of a Hallmark Channel movie, and many of the houses were restored Victorian and Craftsman homes, darling and brightly painted as they stood on Globe's narrow, hilly streets. Over the years—mostly when watching holiday movies on Netflix—I'd sometimes harbored idle dreams of getting out of the L.A. rat race and relocating to such a place, but that's all they'd ever been...daydreams and nothing more.

Well, until today.

Looking at the houses made me realize I needed to research the housing market there. A few minutes on Zillow told me that renting wasn't really an option, since the only things currently available were a junky studio apartment and a very expensive ranch retreat on the edge of town.

No, I'd have to buy something.

That actually wasn't as big an issue as it could have been, since I'd won the lottery a year earlier, thanks to a prosperity spell that had turned out *extremely* well.

Okay, it wasn't as if I'd won a huge Powerball lottery. I wasn't sitting on millions or anything. No, I'd won one of the low-end lotteries, the kind that still left me with a little over three-quarters of a million dollars after taxes. And that, I realized, would buy a heck of a lot of real estate in a place like Globe.

Only...what did I really want to buy? If I was going to sink my not-so-hard-won winnings into a place, I needed to make it count. After all, what was the point in starting over again if I wasn't *really* starting over? If I got something I didn't love, then I knew I wouldn't be emotionally invested enough to make it work.

At first glance, there wasn't a lot to love. A few of the houses looked as though they had potential, but did I want to spend the next six months or more with my bathrooms and kitchens torn up while they were brought into the twenty-first century? My star chart had me pinned as a Gemini, but I was right on the cusp of Cancer, and that meant I tended to be a homebody. Throw in both a moon and ascendant in Libra, and that made me even more averse to any kind of chaos in my environment.

So…I needed something basically turn-key. And there didn't seem to be much like that in Globe. Well, not for someone as picky as I was. Sure, you could argue that a woman on the run didn't have the luxury of being too choosy, but I knew my limitations, and that was definitely one of them. My Libra moon had me making Pinterest boards of all sorts of interior decorating schemes, and I already had in my head what I thought of as my "dream" house, even though I'd never seriously thought about buying a place. Those Lotto winnings would have gotten me a small condo on the Westside of Los Angeles… most likely a fixer-upper. I just couldn't see myself blowing all that money on something that wouldn't make me happy, which was why I'd stayed in my rent-controlled duplex despite having a chunk of change in the bank.

But at least I already had a good idea of what I thought would make me happy.

I went back to Zillow and selected "all" housing types rather than just houses, town-houses, and condos. And boom, there it was.

"Unique live-work space" read the ad. From what I could tell, the place was a storefront with a loft space above it. Everything looked as though it had been recently rehabbed and refurbished. And although I wasn't sure whether living on Globe's main drag was really my first choice, I had to admit that the busiest street in that small town was probably quieter than my own neighborhood in West L.A.

Also, even though I'd never admitted my desire to anyone, thinking it had to be forever out of reach, I'd always secretly wanted to have my own New Age/witchy store, similar to Mazey's Crescent City. Every time I walked in that shop, I had a smile on my face, and I thought it would be amazing to have a place of my own like that.

True, my only retail experience was a disastrous two months working at the local Kohl's when I was a senior in high school, but I figured it would be different if I were running my own store.

Whether or not there was even a market for a New Age shop in sleepy little Globe remained to be seen. After all, a brief Wikipedia search wasn't enough to give me much of a feel for the place. But it was definitely the best prospect I'd seen, and while I usually took a long time to make a major decision like this one, weighing the various pros and cons until I felt comfortable with my choice, I knew I didn't have the luxury of reflection in this particular instance. Not because I was too worried about someone snapping up the property before I could get to it—from what I could tell, the place had been on the market for almost six months—but because I had no idea when Lucien Dumond might decide to make his grudge *very* up close and personal.

Before I could start to hedge, I filled out the contact form on the listing and sent it. There. I'd done all I could. For all I knew, the shop/loft wasn't even available anymore, and the real estate agency had just neglected to take down the ad.

But even as I got up to fetch my neglected cup of tea, my phone rang from inside my purse. I hurried over to grab it and noticed right away that the area code was an unfamiliar one, definitely not anything in the L.A. area.

Again, I made myself answer rather than

letting it roll over to voicemail. Trying to sound cheery and brisk, I said, "Hi, this is Selena Marx."

"Oh, hello, Selena!" exclaimed a woman's voice, gushing, almost theatrical. "This is Josie Woodrow, the listing agent for the property on Broad Street in Globe. I just got your email. When would you like to look at the property?"

"Well...." I hesitated, wondering if there was some way to say I wanted to buy it sight unseen without sounding like a lunatic.

Probably not.

Obviously sensing my hesitation, Josie sailed right in before I had a chance to say anything more. "Oh, I understand that you'd be coming from out of state. My schedule is *very* flexible."

"Thanks," I replied, although the flexibility of Josie Woodrow's schedule really wasn't the point. "No, I actually wanted to know if you had a video walk-through of the place. If I like it, I'll take it."

A long pause on the other end of the line. Then she said, "Well, I don't have one at the moment, but I can pop down there and film a virtual tour on my phone and send it to you. Would that work?"

"It would be great," I replied, hoping I hadn't just shot myself in the foot. What if the walk-through revealed flaws that the still images on the Zillow listing hadn't revealed? Then I'd have to decline and feel guilty for making Josie go to all that extra effort….

But apparently, she wasn't too concerned about the property's possible shortcomings, because she said, "I can go do it right now. Just give me a half hour or so."

"Oh, there's no hurry," I said automatically, even though there sort of was. However, since I couldn't really tell her that I needed to get out of L.A. as quickly as possible because a rabid necromancer had decided he didn't want me operating in the same town—well, without her thinking I was a complete loon—I only added, "But thanks. I really appreciate it."

"No problem at all. I'll send you the video when it's ready. 'Bye!"

She hung up then, and I was left standing there as I stared down at the phone in my hand and wondered if I might have taken leave of my senses.

The die was cast, though, and so there wasn't much I could do except pour myself another cup of tea and try to look around and take a quick inventory of my possessions. The situation seemed to require stealth, and so it wasn't as though I could have a moving pod deposited in front of the house so I could pack my things at my leisure.

And really, I wasn't so attached to my stuff that I couldn't leave most of it behind. Obviously,

I'd take my books and my crystals and favorite pieces of art, along with the items on my altar, as well as my clothes and jewelry. But most of the furniture was thrift store and garage sale finds. I didn't need to take it with me. A few discreet ads on Craigslist, and I could probably get rid of most of it without much of a problem.

As for my clients...well, if I told them I was moving out of state, I'd be tipping my hand, and word might get back to Lucien. Probably better just to say I'd decided to get out of the psychic business, and then give them referrals to other witches in the area that I knew could take them on as clients and provide the kind of readings they expected.

And family?

Well, my mother and I weren't very close. It wasn't that we had an acrimonious relationship, more like, since I'd proved to her that I was able to support myself from the time I was nineteen, she didn't see a huge reason to be intimately involved in my life. My choice of vocation had bemused her more than anything else, although I knew that when she spoke about me to her husband's friends, she always referred to me as a "life coach." I guessed that "hedgewitch" wouldn't go over too well at cocktail parties. Yes, L.A. had its share of New Age types, but most people didn't think magic was real.

I knew better, however.

Anyway, if I told my mother that I'd decided to move to Arizona, she would probably take the news calmly in stride just like she did just about everything else in life. Even an unexpected pregnancy at twenty-three hadn't really thrown her for a loop. No, Elizabeth Marx just kept on keeping on.

In a way, I wished I could be more like her. Nothing ever seemed to rattle her cage.

Whereas I was seriously planning on upheaving my life because of a rumor.

No, it was more than that. If Mazey had only been telling tales out of school—which really wasn't her style—then the cards and the pendulum would have shown me it was safe to disregard her warnings. Instead, they'd pointed me toward a new beginning in a new place. And that meant I was probably doing the right thing, even if it might have seemed crazy to an outside observer.

My phone beeped, signaling that I had a text. I unlocked the screen and went to my messages, then opened up the attached video Josie had sent. It was a little jerky, probably because she'd been hurrying, but it showed me pretty much everything I'd wanted to see.

The place was beautiful. Old wood floors sanded to a soft gloss, high ceilings with probably the original plaster moldings. Exposed brick on one wall framing a real fireplace with a honey-oak mantel. The kitchen was small but had granite counters and new-looking stainless appliances. Both bathrooms were likewise updated and gorgeous. Two bedrooms with high ceilings and surprisingly ample closet space—a lot more than I had in my current duplex.

And the storefront downstairs was equally nice. The walls had been faux-finished in a warm reddish umber, and there were more of the same moldings and exposed brick. No display fixtures, but I could order all that stuff once I'd determined what kind of stock I'd be selling.

All in all, I probably couldn't have found a better place to land if I'd chosen everything myself. If this wasn't the universe telling me that Globe was the place I was meant to go, I didn't know what else it could possibly be. The nervous churn in my stomach subsided a little, and I took a breath. I knew what I needed to do.

Love it, I texted Josie. *I'll take it. I'm paying cash; what's the next step?*

For some reason, I'd expected another flabbergasted pause. This time, however, she seemed to be ready for me, because she came back immediately.

You'll need a ready cash deposit to hold the place, she responded. *Then an inspection and a title search. I can set all that up. Once it's done, you'll need to send a cashier's check or wire the funds. I can walk you through all that.*

Great, I told her. *Go ahead and let me know where to send the deposit.*

She texted over the information, and I told her I'd get it to her as quickly as possible. In fact, as soon as I was done messaging her, I called my bank and requested the wire transfer for the deposit. Not too long after that, I got another text from Josie, letting me know the wire transfer had gone through and she was in the process of reaching out to the house inspector.

The place will be yours in less than a week, she messaged. *Start packing!*

When I saw that text, my hands started to shake. I'd done some crazy, impulsive things in my life, but buying a live/work space in Globe, Arizona, sight unseen probably had to sit at the top of that list.

To reassure myself, I pulled out my Tarot deck again and gave it a good shuffle. I didn't know what I'd do if the damn thing turned up another Tower card, but I needed to know.

The Ace of Pentacles. Probably one of the most fortuitous cards to turn up in the deck, it generally symbolized wealth and opportunity. I didn't know if I was going to strike it rich selling pagan paraphernalia in small-town Arizona, but it seemed I wouldn't have to worry too much about taking a financial bath.

Just to be sure, though....

I pulled another card.

The Lovers. Hmm.

Other than Lucien's completely unwanted physical interest in me, I hadn't had much of what you could call luck in the romantic sense. I was always upfront with the guys I dated, telling them how I earned a living and how my metaphysical practices were a huge part of my life, but they tended to bail out as soon as I told them I couldn't go to the movies that night because I had to stay home and recharge my crystals under the light of a full moon.

A pursuit of any kind of love life hadn't been my motivation for moving to Arizona, but if that's what it took to get things to make a turn for the better, I supposed I'd roll with it. I tried to imagine what kind of guy I'd even meet in Globe. Some sort of cowboy type, maybe. There were still working ranches in the area. Or a biker...one of the pictures I'd pulled up in my Google search of Globe had been of a downtown bar called the Drift Inn that had an impressive lineup of Harleys parked in front of it.

Both cowboys and bikers had been in pretty short supply in my life. I hadn't really imagined myself with either type, but if that was what the universe wanted to throw at me....

Feeling far more hopeful than I'd been a few minutes earlier, I reshuffled the Tarot deck and slid it into its protective velvet pouch. That task done, I stood up and surveyed my living room once again.

This was going to take a lot of work. I had to hope I was up to it.

3

Cats and Curses

JOSIE WOODROW TURNED OUT TO BE A PLUMP bundle of perpetual motion, topped by fiery red hair cut into a messy bob. She beamed as she handed the keys of my new home over to me.

"I had my own cleaning gal go through and give everything a once-over, since the place has been sitting empty so long," she said, standing off to one side as I stood in the center of what would become my store.

To my relief, the place looked even better in person. Or maybe it was only that now I was there in the flesh, so to speak, I could breathe in the vibes of the building, could feel it welcome me to the space. Some people might have said that was my imagination and nothing more, but I knew better. I'd always been sensitive to the vibrations in houses and buildings, and this one was no exception. People had been happy here during the building's long life.

I had to hope I would be, too.

"It's hard to imagine someone giving this place up after all the work that was put into it," I remarked, and Josie let out a sad little sigh.

"I know. But Alison—the owner—had to move back to Rhode Island after her mother's stroke. At first, she thought she might rent out the place, but then she decided it would be too much work trying to manage a rental property from all the way across the country. So she put it on the market."

I walked toward the back wall, already envisioning it covered in shelves filled with jars of herbs and essential oils. "What was she going to do with it?"

"Oh, she was going to make it into a tearoom —you know, someplace where you could come and have finger sandwiches and little desserts, that sort of thing." Another of those expressive sighs, and Josie's pudgy shoulders lifted slightly. "I was looking forward to it…not that I don't think your shop sounds very nice," she added quickly, obviously not wanting to offend me by allowing me to think she didn't approve of a New Age shop in the middle of Globe's downtown.

"I hope it will be," I said. "First, I'll get the apartment settled, and then I'll work on putting the shop together." Pausing there, I inspected the faux-washed, warm-hued walls and frowned a little.

Josie's expression immediately shifted to one of concern. "Is there something wrong?"

"No," I replied. I definitely didn't want her to think I'd found fault with the place. "It's just that I was thinking of calling the shop 'Once in a Blue Moon,' and so I'm not sure these red walls are going to work."

"Oh," she said, and let out a relieved little chuckle. "I know a very good painter. I can text you his contact information."

I reflected that it was helpful to have made contact with the one person who seemed to know everyone in Globe. Not that I couldn't have tackled the painting myself if necessary, but it was probably better to let an expert handle it so I could focus on ordering display items and inventory for the store.

"That would be great."

She fished an oversized iPhone out of her purse—a brand-new one, from what I could tell, several generations newer and fancier than mine—and typed a quick text. Almost immediately, my own phone pinged from within my purse.

"Brett Woodrow?" I said, inspecting the text after I'd extracted my own iPhone.

Her cheeks flushed a little pinker under the

blush she wore. "My nephew. But he really is the best house painter in town. And I know he just finished up a big project at a ranch just over in Miami, so he should be available."

I'd have to take her word for it. But then, it wasn't as if I knew anyone else in Globe. I would've had to resort to Yelp or Angie's List to find a painter in town, so I might as well go with Josie's recommendation.

"Sounds perfect," I told her, then slid my phone back into my purse. "I'll get in touch after I'm a bit more settled."

"I'll let him know to expect a call from you," she replied. "And speaking of getting settled in, I'll leave you to it. If you have any problems or questions, just text or call."

"I will," I promised, although I didn't foresee any issues arising. Everything looked to be in perfect order, and I'd bought a homeowner's warranty just to cover my butt in case the furnace decided to blow up or something.

Josie shot another smile at me, then went ahead and let herself out. The door to the shop closed behind her with a quiet *snick,* and I took a deep breath in as I looked around.

For better or worse, I was home.

I'd put what I could in my Beetle—clothes and personal items—but everything else had been shipped directly to the new place. The expense had been pretty cringe-worthy, although I told myself that putting my books and crystals and art and all the other items I couldn't leave behind in plain brown boxes and sending them via UPS had been really the only way to keep my move on the down-low.

The only person who knew where I was going was my mother. Telling her had been a calculated risk, but it wasn't as though I could just take off for the wild west without letting my only living relative know where I was going. I wouldn't fool myself into thinking that Lucien Dumond didn't know who she was and where she lived—and I wasn't too happy that his compound in the Encino hills stood only a few miles away from the sprawling house in Sherman Oaks that my mother shared with her husband—and yet I tried to convince myself that Dumond had no reason to go after her. I'd been the main thorn in his side, and since I'd plucked the thorn and removed myself from Southern California, he could live happy in the knowledge that no one would be competing with him when it came to peddling his services to desperate starlets.

My new loft apartment was now littered with boxes. All I had to sleep on was an inflatable mattress I'd ordered from Amazon just so I wouldn't be lying on the floor while I waited for my new furniture to show up. All that had been ordered online as well, and would be arriving in dribs and drabs over the next few days.

Looking at all those boxes could have been overwhelming, but I'd done a quick reading right before I got out of the car, and the universe still seemed to be telling me that all systems were go. Yes, I had a lot of work in front of me. Still, it wasn't as if I had any sort of timeline for when everything needed to be in place, so I could feel my way through it and get things done in my own time.

In a way, it was oddly satisfying to think that I didn't have a schedule ruling my life, that I could completely call my time my own. Oh, I'd loved working with my clients, and had experienced quite a few pangs of guilt as I let all of them know I was closing down my practice, even as I'd done my best to guide them to new practitioners, but it still felt as though an invisible weight had been lifted from my shoulders.

I'd brought my teakettle with me and made sure it was in a clearly labeled box. After fetching the pair of kitchen shears I'd left out on the counter, I sliced through the tape holding the box shut and got out the ocean-blue Le Creuset kettle that had been one of my splurges a while back.

Soon enough, it was whistling away happily on the stove, and not so long after that, I had my first cup of tea—Assam—in my new home.

The same feeling of peace and harmony that I'd sensed down in the store space filled the loft apartment as well, and I pulled in a deep, calming breath, letting myself relax into my surroundings. I walked through the space, ignoring the chaos of boxes around me and instead doing my best to focus on the way the light tracked along the gleaming wood floors, the way the dust motes danced in the sunlight that filtered through the tall windows on the east side of the living room.

That stillness was abruptly broken by a scratching noise coming from somewhere toward the back of the space, followed by a peremptory *meow.*

What the…?

I set down my mug of tea and hurried toward the back bedroom—the master bedroom, I supposed, since it was the larger of the two and had its own balcony overlooking a not-so-scenic empty lot.

Standing on the balcony and staring through the French door that opened onto it was a large gray cat. It glared at me with huge yellow eyes and meowed again.

Obviously, it wanted in.

Growing up, I'd had a big black and white

kitty. Star Ruby, a name my five-year-old self had thought was just perfect for a male cat. Star had been my constant companion all the way up to my senior year of high school, when he passed away after a long and happy life. I'd wanted to get another cat after I moved out, but a series of overly strict landlords had kept that from happening. Over time, I'd gotten used to my cat-less existence, and yet I'd always secretly hoped that one day I'd be living someplace where I could have a cat again.

Well, it seemed as if a cat had literally just turned up on my doorstep.

It doesn't necessarily mean anything, I told myself as I went over to the door. *This could be a neighbor's cat just poking around.*

Possibly, except I didn't really have any neighbors. Oh, there were businesses to either side—a furniture store and an antique/junk shop—but Josie had told me that no one lived in the apartments above those stores, that the shop owners used them for storage.

Still, cats could range a good ways if they were in the mood.

I opened the door, and the cat immediately entered the bedroom, tail held high, walking as if he owned the place. Smiling a little, I watched as he strolled toward the doorway that opened onto the hall, then paused to rub up against the frame, getting in a good back scratch, marking it with his scent. Afterward, he continued toward the living room before he stopped in the middle of the chaos, eyes narrowing.

Was that cat *judging* me?

I followed him, then paused, hands planted on my hips. "Hey, I just moved in," I said. Back in the day, I'd always talked to Star like he was a person, and I saw no reason to change that behavior now. "It'll be great when I'm done."

Could a cat arch an eyebrow? His tail flicked from side to side, and then he said in bored tones, "I'll believe it when I see it."

My eyes widened. Had that cat just talked to me?

No, I had to be imagining things. I'd been up since five that morning, wanting to get out of L.A. before the traffic turned truly hideous. I was just tired.

"I assure you, I am talking," he went on, as if in response to the surprised look I must have been wearing. Definitely a male voice, too, slightly contemptuous, as if he just couldn't be bothered with my incredulity. "My name is Archie. And you are?"

"S-selena Marx," I stammered, wondering if the strain of the move had all been too much. Did you know you were having a psychotic break while you were having it?

"Hello, Selena," he said. "I was hoping someone would move in here. It's been quite dull loitering around here and depending on handouts."

Since it seemed I was going to have a conversation with the cat, no matter how crazy such a prospect might have seemed, I figured I might as well roll with it. "This is your house?"

"I've made it my house," Archie replied, which didn't seem like much of an answer at all.

Probably better not to press him on it. "Do you talk to anyone else?"

"No one else in this town is a witch," he said. "Therefore, I can't talk to them."

He made his situation sound so plausible. Maybe it was.

"Good to know," I said lightly. "So…why can you talk to witches? Because I used to have a cat, and I know for a fact that he never talked to me, as much as I might have wanted him to."

"Because I'm not *really* a cat," Archie responded, now sounding slightly irritated. "I was cursed to be a cat. And let me tell you—spending your days scrounging out of garbage cans and licking your own rear end is definitely a curse."

Somehow, I managed to clamp my lips shut before a snicker could escape them. "I suppose I can see that," I said, trying to keep my voice level. "So, you used to be human?"

"I'm still human *inside*," he returned point-edly. "I just look like a cat."

Of course. Then again, I wasn't sure I liked the idea of having a human man trapped inside a cat's body hanging around my new house. The situation could be awkward, to say the least.

The Goddess only knows what my face looked like right then. My expression must have shifted, because Archie went on, now sounding downright irritated, "I certainly would have no designs on your person even if I were still in my human form. My interests lie elsewhere."

"You're gay?" I asked, figuring that would be just about par for the course. Naturally, I'd end up someplace haunted by a cat that used to be a gay man.

"I am asexual," he said primly. "Not that we had such a name for it back in the day. I only knew that I wasn't interested in anyone…which is why I ended up in this ridiculous predicament. The witch who put this curse on me didn't want to believe I couldn't be enticed by her charms."

That must have been a hell of a curse. Honestly, I wasn't sure I would have believed such a thing was possible…except that I was standing in the middle of my new living room, having a conversation with a cat.

"What happened to the witch?" I honestly did want to know, because everything I'd read and every belief I held dear about the craft dictated that casting curses was a very bad idea, that whatever evil you put out into the world would come back to you threefold.

"She was run over by a Packard," Archie replied, then added before I could comment, "I have been a cat for a *very* long time."

Apparently. When was the last time people regularly drove Packards? Long before either I or my mother was born, that's for sure...and probably before even my grandmother was born.

But the curse-casting witch's fate seemed to tell me that my beliefs about casting hexes were valid. At the same time, I had to feel sorry for poor Archie, consigned to an animal's body for decades and decades.

"Well, you're certainly welcome here," I said, knowing I wasn't going to cast him out into the cold, even if I had never planned on having a talking cat as a companion. The poor guy needed shelter, a place he could call his own. "But I suppose that means I'll have to go out and get you some supplies. I don't have a litter box or anything."

"An indoor bathroom," he said then, and looked almost wistful. "That would be a nice change of pace."

Well, I'd been planning to go out and get

stocks of toilet paper and Kleenex and other odds and ends anyway. "Any pet stores in town?"

"I don't believe so. There's a Walmart."

Back in L.A., I would never set foot inside a Walmart. I'd always been a Target girl. But now that I was in Globe, I realized I didn't have a lot of options…unless I wanted to drive all the way into Queen Creek or Mesa, two of Phoenix's most southeastern suburbs.

I tried not to sigh. "Okay. Do you want me to get you a bowl of water before I head out?"

"And some salmon treats?" he asked hopefully.

"The cupboard is bare," I said. "I was planning to go to the store after I did some work here."

"Water will have to do, then."

Luckily, I'd brought along a few odds and ends of dishes to tide me over until the ones I'd ordered showed up. I got out a bowl, rinsed it off, and then filled it with water. As soon as I set it on the floor, Archie ambled over and began to drink. He seemed relaxed about the whole thing, but I could tell he must have been pretty thirsty.

How long had he been out on the balcony, just waiting for me to show up?

Poor guy.

I resisted the impulse to reach down and scratch him behind the ears. After all, we didn't know each other that well yet.

"Be back soon," I promised him, and he yawned and headed out to the living room.

"Get me a bed and a scratching post, too."

Hmm. I was starting to get the impression that Archie had a bit of an entitlement complex. However, since I'd already agreed to take him in, I figured there was no point in arguing.

After all, it wasn't as if I couldn't afford to get him a few odds and ends.

I let myself out, wondering all the while what else Globe had in store for me.

The trip to Walmart turned out to be fairly uneventful, though, and I was back at my new home within the hour. It took a while to lug all my purchases up to the second floor, but eventually, Archie was gifted with the requested cat bed and scratching post, and had wolfed down a bowl of Special Kitty dry cat food. Thus fortified, he curled up in a ball and promptly went to sleep in a patch of sunlight slipping through the window of the second bedroom, the one I planned to turn into an office.

While I was out, I'd gotten a text from the place where I'd bought my living room furniture that delivery had been updated to the next day. Perfect. I didn't know why the schedule had been shifted by three days, but I wasn't going to argue. I hadn't been looking forward to sitting on a folding chair until my new furniture showed up, and now I wouldn't have to worry about it.

I also heard from Josie's nephew Brett, who wanted to know if he could stop by and take a look at the place so he could give me an estimate. It seemed like a perfectly logical request, so I told him that would be fine. Although I wasn't in any rush, I still wanted to see what the shop space would look like once the warm reddish faux finish had been replaced by cool blue.

From the way he eyed me as he entered the place, I had a feeling I wasn't what he'd been expecting. I also noticed the glint of a wedding ring on his left hand, so apparently, he wasn't the "love connection" the cards had predicted for me in Globe.

Which was fine. I still hadn't quite come to terms with having a cursed asexual cat living in my apartment, and so I probably didn't need the complication of a love life quite yet.

Besides, Brett, while not bad-looking, wasn't really my type. His hair was just as blazing red as his aunt's, telling me that even if she was helping nature along at this point, her fiery hair had started out natural enough, and he had a redhead's freckled complexion and stood barely an inch taller than I did. My taste tended to lean more toward the tall, dark, and handsome type, although there hadn't been much of that in my life lately.

At any rate, since I was wearing faded jeans, lime green Keds, and a green cardigan over a white T-shirt, I guessed I didn't look quite like the woo-woo shop owner Brett had been expecting.

"Just this space?" he asked, looking around the store area.

"Yes," I said. "The upstairs is great. Actually, the paint here normally would be fine, but it won't work with the theme of the store."

A nod and a businesslike "got it," and Brett took a quick survey, going up close and running a hand over the walls to make sure there weren't any hidden spots that might need repair.

"Eight hundred," he announced when he was done, which sounded reasonable to me. "I've got some swatches—I'll need to go into Mesa to get the paint, since there isn't anything closer with a decent variety."

For the next few minutes, I pored over the swatch books he provided, then said I wanted "Moonlit Indigo," which was a darkish blue with a faint green undertone. He nodded and told me he'd be back the next day, we shook hands, and that, it seemed, was that.

Archie was still sleeping when I went upstairs, so I puttered around and made a decent dent in the stacked boxes in the living room and master bedroom. By the time he woke up, the place didn't look quite so much like a disaster area, although of course, it wouldn't really begin to resemble a home until the furniture started to arrive.

"Why did you leave all your furniture behind?" he asked as I put a frozen dinner in the microwave to heat up. Thank the Goddess that the kitchen had one of those built-in units above the stove, or I would've been forced to get takeout somewhere. Trying some of the local restaurants was something I planned to do in the not-too-distant future, but right then, I was just too tired to even contemplate going back out.

"Garage sale stuff that wasn't worth moving," I said briefly as I reached for the bottle of chardonnay I'd bought at Walmart.

It couldn't really be classified as drinking alone if I had a talking cat for company, right?

Archie absorbed my reply and appeared to decide it wasn't worth further investigation. He looked at the wine I was pouring into a glass and let out a sound suspiciously like a sigh.

"I'd pour you some," I told him, "except I doubt your kitty metabolism could handle it."

The fur on his back arched, and his eyes slitted. "Don't," he said, "under any circumstances refer to me as a 'kitty.'"

"Duly noted."

He stalked off into the living room, and I allowed myself a sip of chardonnay. Not bad. Actually, I'd been sort of surprised by how good the wine selection at the local Walmart was. It seemed like I might not have ended up in as much of a backwater as I'd feared.

The microwave beeped, and I pulled out my tray of Lean Cuisine pasta carbonara. Under ordinary circumstances, I wouldn't have eaten anything like that—frozen meals tended to be pumped full of sodium and preservatives—but if I was too tired to go on the hunt for takeout, that meant I was doubly incapable of actually cooking something.

All I had to sit down on was a canvas folding chair I'd bought a few years earlier to take to summer concerts in the park. It was already set up in the living room, so I went ahead and took a seat, balancing the Lean Cuisine tray on one leg since I didn't have anywhere else to put it. Another sip of chardonnay, and then I set the glass on the floor.

Archie gave it a jaundiced look but didn't move from his spot near the windows. For a few minutes, I ate in silence. Then I asked, "Did you ever get anyone to try to break the curse?"

"Who?" he said derisively. "I already told you, there aren't any other witches in this town."

"Well, now," I replied, even as I realized that wasn't precisely true, since I was now a resident of Globe. But that was a very recent occurrence. "I mean, not even the whole time you've been in a cat's form?"

He reached up to scratch behind one ear with a hind paw, then settled back down on the floor. The bare wood didn't look very comfortable, and I was glad that a new rug would be arriving the next day with a bunch of my furniture.

"The witch who cursed me was the only one," he said. "I suppose after that Packard flattened her, word got around that Globe wasn't a very safe place for witches."

And here I'd decided to make it my new hometown. But I was obviously a very different kind of witch from the one who'd stolen his human form from him, so I had to hope I'd be okay.

When I didn't say anything right away, he went on, "I don't suppose you'd want to give it a try."

Could I even attempt such a feat? My magic had always been contained in small, safe things—casting spells of banishment and protection, using divination to give people advice on their futures and their relationships. Turning a cat back into a man was an order of magnitude greater than anything I'd ever heard of.

Or maybe several orders of magnitude.

"I don't know if that's something I can do," I admitted. "I'm just a hedgewitch."

His tail whipped back and forth in annoyance. "What's a hedgewitch?"

"Someone self-trained, who doesn't work with a coven," I replied. "Someone who practices small magics. But," I hurried to add, "that doesn't mean I can't do some research and see if I can dig up anything that would help you...once I get settled."

I could tell he didn't much like the idea of the sort of delay waiting until I had everything put together might cause, but it seemed he didn't want to argue, because he grudgingly responded, "All right," and closed his eyes.

Maybe he was asleep, or maybe he was just sulking. Either way, I needed to finish my makeshift meal.

As I picked up the glass of chardonnay and took a sip, I reflected that my first night in Globe was definitely nothing I could have ever expected.

4

Opening Night

THAT FIRST DAY TURNED INTO ANOTHER DAY, and then another. Before too long, the apartment was fully furnished, and I had to admit I probably enjoyed all that new furniture more than I should have. Yes, there was something to be said for antiques, for pieces that had been previously loved and which had absorbed the unique energies of their former owners...but there was also a lot to be said for having tables without burn marks from careless cigarette butts or scratches from too many moves.

As I'd promised Archie, I tried to do some research on spells that might get him out of his predicament, but so far, I hadn't found very much. Most of the spells contained in my own books of magic were confined to benign topics like healing and abundance enchantments, and while the darker texts might have provided some information on how to turn someone into a toad—or a cat—they were pretty unhelpful about offering any actionable data on how to turn someone back.

Oddly enough, my unexpected roommate and I got along better than I'd thought we would. He had me put the cat bed in the second bedroom/office, and since I didn't spend a huge amount of time in there, it wasn't as though we tripped over each other much. He also had a tendency to slip out as soon as I opened the front door so he could wander the neighborhood. How he'd managed to avoid getting hit by a car or eaten by coyotes all those years, I had no idea, but I supposed there was something to be said for having a human brain in a cat body.

I asked him one time why no one had ever noticed that the same gray cat had been lurking around the area for decades, and he'd only tilted his head at me.

"People see what they want to see," he replied, a cryptic comment that didn't do much to illuminate the situation but which, I realized later, was only the truth. And since he'd turned out to be an unobtrusive companion—at least I never had to worry about him lurking near the bathroom, trying to sneak a peek as I got out of the shower—I figured he could keep his secrets. After being cursed to remain in a cat's body for sixty years or more, he'd probably earned that right.

The same week I moved in, Brett came over and turned the downstairs shop space into the azure haven I'd envisioned, and he also told me about a local artist who did beautiful murals and sign painting. I got in touch with Hazel Marr, the artist in question—who turned out to be only a few years older than I was, and someone I felt comfortable with right away—and she transformed the shop ceiling into a gorgeous night sky adorned with all the constellations of the zodiac, along with a beautiful crescent moon above the front door.

Ordering display cases and tables, along with all the various items I wanted to sell in the shop, took a bit more time. Still, less than a month had passed by the time I was ready to open Once in a Blue Moon to the public.

Josie advised me to have a grand opening, with drinks and snacks. "People are curious about the place, of course," she said one afternoon when she dropped by to see how everything was progressing. "But booze really helps to get them in the door."

I couldn't help laughing at her comment, although I had a feeling she was right. "If that's what it takes," I replied, thinking that the food and drinks would be a good tax write-off, if nothing else. "And I'd love it if you could help me get the word out."

"Consider it done," she told me.

And that was why, when I officially opened the doors to Once in a Blue Moon on Friday, April ninth, I immediately had a flood of people coming inside. Josie, of course, and her nephew Brett, accompanied by a slight, fair-haired woman I guessed was his wife. I'd learned earlier that Josie had been divorced for years and had no intention of remarrying—"why would I waste my time on that nonsense?" she asked rhetorically during one of her visits—and with her came Hazel, the artist, who I'd already gotten friendly with as she worked on the shop ceiling. I had a feeling Hazel was glad to see someone a little left of center show up in town—the streaks in her light brown hair varied with her mood, and were blue and pink that particular night, and she also had a tiny diamond stud in her nose—while I knew I was certainly happy to have met a woman around my own age who didn't give me the side-eye when I casually announced I was a practicing witch. We were a long ways past the bad old days of the Salem witch trials, but a lot of people still weren't super-comfortable with the whole woo-woo thing.

More people arrived after that: the two guys from the coffee house down the street, and Max, the gruff individual who owned the antique store right next to my shop. And still more Globe residents I didn't recognize, all of them looking friendly enough, even though I noticed a few of them giving sketchy glances at the items engraved with pentacles or the sacred triple moon, like my mini cauldrons and carved altar pieces.

Still, no one had shown up with torches and pitchforks, and so I figured I could already count the evening a success because of that. People sipped from little plastic cups of wine and ate cheese and crackers and fruit, and some of them even bought a few things. The essential oils and candles seemed especially popular, and I made a mental note that I'd probably have to restock those items more frequently.

And then *he* walked in.

I was so focused on his handsome, strongly marked features and the long, night-black hair pulled back into a severe ponytail that at first, I didn't even realize he was wearing a uniform of some sort. Cop? I supposed so, but the members of the Globe P.D. that I'd spotted during my time in town had worn dark blue uniforms, while this stranger's was khaki.

"Calvin Standingbear," came Josie's voice at my ear, and I turned to see her standing a foot behind me, a knowing smile on her face. "He's the police chief for the San Ramon Apache tribe. They operate the casino just down the road."

Right. I vaguely recalled seeing a turnoff for a casino when I was out exploring in my Beetle, but because gambling had never been my thing, I hadn't paid it very much attention. And I knew I'd seen people shopping at the Walmart in Globe that I guessed had to be Native American, although I didn't know anything about the local tribe.

"I hope he's not here to check for a liquor license or something," I joked. Josie had assured me that as long as I was giving the wine away and not expecting people to purchase anything in exchange, I should be fine, but my stomach did a nervous flip-flop anyway.

Or maybe that was simply how my body had decided to react to the godlike specimen who'd just entered the shop.

She waved a hand. "Oh, the tribal police don't have jurisdiction here in town. No, he probably dropped by to take a look because he was curious. People have been talking about this place since you moved in."

"I had no idea I was such a topic of conversation."

All right, my comment was probably a little disingenuous. No, I'd never grown up in a small town, but I knew my arrival had caused something of a flutter in Globe, if only because a town that size didn't get a lot of people moving in, and to have someone show up and buy a highly visible property sight unseen—and for cash, no less—would naturally start tongues wagging.

How did they know I'd paid cash for my live/work space? Because I might not have been around all that long, but I'd already learned that Josie was a world-class gossip. She tended to slide tidbits about people and their goings-on into conversations, coming at them sideways rather than making a full-blown announcement, and yet it was pretty obvious that it would be hard to have any secrets in my new hometown.

Not that I had many to keep. True, I hadn't gone around blurting out that the cat I'd adopted was actually a cursed human in disguise, but otherwise, people pretty much already knew the worst about me…or at least, what they would have considered the worst. After all, if I'd wanted to hide the fact that I was a practicing witch, I probably wouldn't have opened a big ol' pagan shop right in Globe's historic downtown.

All I got in response to my comment was a knowing smile from Josie. And then—to my chagrin—she raised a hand and called out, "Calvin! Come over and meet Selena!"

I wanted to sink through the newly polished floor. Instead, I managed to stand there and did my best to look interested in a neutral, completely nonsexual sort of way as he walked over to me.

Once he got closer, I realized how tall he really was. I stood five foot eight in my stocking feet, so I wasn't exactly what you could call short, but it still seemed as though he towered over me.

A friendly smile crinkled his dark eyes, showing a few laugh lines around them. "Hello, Selena," he said. His voice was deep, and he spoke in a deliberate sort of way, as if he considered each word before releasing it into the wild. "The shop looks very nice."

Utterly prosaic words, and yet they started my heart beating at a ridiculous pace. Yes, ridiculous. I was a grown woman who'd be turning thirty in two months. I shouldn't be reacting to a man—all right, a pretty magnificent specimen, but still— like I was some seventh-grader getting asked to dance for the first time.

"Thank you," I responded. Josie had said he was the chief of police on the reservation. Did that mean I should call him Chief Standingbear? It was his formal title, but I had a feeling I would sound like an idiot if I said the words out loud. Probably better not to say his name at all. "Brett and Hazel really helped to make my vision come to life."

Oh, Goddess, that sounded so pretentious. I wished I could bite my tongue, but since the damage was done, I thought it was probably best just to hurry on and hope he hadn't noticed.

"Would you like a glass of wine?" I asked.

"Not while I'm in uniform," he said, and again, an awkward flush rushed to my cheeks. Damn, I really was making a hash of things, wasn't I? But before I could stammer an apology, he went on, "I'll get myself some water. Thanks for the offer, though."

I nodded and tried to smile. Josie stepped in then, saying, "Calvin, I heard a rumor that the tribe is thinking of canceling the poker tournament next month. Tell me that isn't true."

Maybe his mouth quirked ever so slightly at the overly tragic tone of her voice. "We've been discussing it. Attendance has dropped off the past few years, and we're wondering if it's still worth the effort."

"But it brings so much to the town," she protested. "Maybe all you need to do is advertise a bit more."

His expression didn't change. "I'll bring it up with the elders. We're going to have to make a decision soon, either way."

Josie's bright blue eyes lit up in a way that I was already learning to dread. "You should have Selena cast an abundance charm for you!"

"I don't think—" I began, but she waved a hand, even as the twitch at the corner of Calvin's mouth turned into a lopsided smile.

"I'll take it under advisement," he said, then

nodded toward me. "Nice to meet you, Selena. You've got a great store here."

And before either I or Josie could say anything else, he headed off toward the refreshments.

I tried to keep the accusation out of my voice as I remarked, "Well, that could've gone better."

Another of those dismissive hand waves. "Oh, it went fine. I think he likes you."

"I kind of doubt that."

She chuckled. "Oh, but I know Cal, and you don't. He's not the type to give compliments if they're not justified. I can tell he's impressed with the store." Her voice lowered, and she added, "He's single, in case you were wondering."

"I wasn't," I said crisply, even though that was a flat-out lie.

"Mm-hmm." Apparently, Josie wasn't buying it, either. "Never married. I don't know why. I guess he was just waiting for the right girl to come along."

Having delivered that remark, she sent me a knowing glance and then headed off toward the refreshment table as well, although—to my relief —she didn't approach Calvin Standingbear, but instead stopped to talk to a couple around her own age, although they weren't nearly as flamboyant.

A woman I didn't know was waiting at the counter, a crystal-embedded healing candle in one hand, so I hurried over to take care of her purchase. Several other people followed after that, including a pair of girls who looked as though they were probably still in high school. With much giggling, they bought a deck of moon oracle cards and a few of my smaller, less expensive crystals, and I wondered how serious they intended to be about their purchases.

But at least they'd served as a useful distraction, and by the time I was done taking care of them, I looked up to find that Calvin Standing-bear had already left the building. I couldn't quite prevent the stab of disappointment that went through me when I realized he was gone, even though I tried to tell myself it was kind of silly to be upset that he hadn't hung around. Even if he had any interest in me—and I had no reason to believe he did—an open house at a New Age store with a few dozen people milling around wasn't exactly the best setup for an intimate conversation.

Hazel Marr came over to the counter, greenish eyes glinting with amusement. "I see you met the resident stud."

"What?" I asked, trying to play dumb.

She crossed her arms with a jingle of silver bangle bracelets. When she wasn't dressed in old jeans and a paint-spattered T-shirt, she could give me a run for the money in the bohemian wardrobe department. Tonight she was wearing a tie-dyed tank dress with a bright pink cardigan on top. "Calvin Standingbear. You were looking at him like a Weight Watchers junkie might stare at a piece of chocolate cake."

So much for trying to act nonchalant. "Was I that obvious?"

"Probably not to everyone," she replied, obviously trying to take pity on me. "But I've felt that same expression on my own face, so I suppose that made it easy to recognize."

"Did you ever go out with him?"

"Calvin? No." She laughed, a rueful little chuckle that couldn't quite hide her disappointment at the situation. "The San Ramon Apache keep to themselves. I mean, they come to town to do their shopping or to go out to eat or have a drink, but they don't mingle much. I'm not a Globe native, but I've lived here for seven years now, and I don't think I've ever heard of any of them dating or marrying one of us honkies."

"'Honkies'?" I repeated.

Hazel grinned. "Well, whatever Native Americans call us white folks. Anyway, I'm pretty sure Calvin's a lost cause, but that doesn't mean I don't try to get an eyeful whenever he crosses my path. Looking never hurt anyone."

No...unless your brain started manufacturing all sorts of unlikely scenarios as a result of that so-called "looking." I wondered what the hell Josie had been thinking by being so transparent in her introductions. During one of our conversations, she'd told me that she was born and raised in Globe, that her family had been there for generations, so it wasn't as if she didn't already know about the standoffish behavior of the San Ramon tribe. Had she somehow thought a witch from L.A. might have a chance where none of the local women had?

Again, not the sort of conversation I wanted to have in that kind of crowd. I filed my questions away for later and said, "I guess I'll join you in looking. So far, I haven't seen a lot of prospects in this town."

Hazel still appeared more amused than anything, so I guessed she wasn't too disappointed by the lack of local dating prospects. "No, if you were looking for hookups, you would've done a lot better to stay in L.A." Her expression turned speculative. "What made you choose Globe?"

There it was. I knew she'd been pondering that question ever since she came over to the shop the first time to give me an estimate for the ceiling murals. Of course, she'd been too polite to come out and ask, but I was sure almost everyone had been wondering the same thing. I'd told Josie that I was tired of Los Angeles and wanted to get out of the big city to someplace where I could see the sky and get some fresh air, but Globe still seemed like an odd choice. Someone with my interests would've done better to move to the New Age haven of Sedona, or even the Verde Valley, which got a lot of tourists because of the wine industry there.

Obviously, I couldn't tell Hazel that I'd ended up in the out-of-the-way mining town because both my pendulum and my Tarot cards had guided me there. Or maybe I could. I'd already gone full woo-woo for everyone to see, so it wasn't as if she'd be terribly surprised by such a revelation.

"The universe guided me here," I said, and to my relief, she smiled and took a sip of Walmart merlot.

"I guess a lot of us can say that about where we've ended up," she replied. "I knew I wanted to be someplace that wasn't touristy, but I wanted a town that was in the mountains, where I'd find something to paint every day."

Well, she'd definitely found it in Globe. Our surroundings weren't as breathtaking as what you'd find in Sedona or Flagstaff—or at least, what I assumed you'd find, based on the photos I'd seen —but mountains rose up in almost every direction, and you didn't have to drive very far to find some truly breathtaking vistas.

"Of course," she went on, "almost any mountain looks good to me, since I grew up in Iowa. Not much more than hills there."

I'd never been to the Midwest, but I still knew she wasn't saying anything more than the truth. Inwardly, I thanked the universe for sending me to a place that had an interesting landscape. After spending my entire life in Southern California, where mountains and hills ranged almost everywhere you looked, I knew I would have felt as though something was missing if I'd ended up in Iowa or Kansas or Oklahoma.

We chatted a bit more, and made plans to meet for lunch the next day at Olamendi's, the Mexican restaurant down the street. Hazel headed off to talk to Bryan and Kris, the guys who ran the coffee shop, and I found myself thankful as well that our paths had crossed. Maybe I didn't have many romantic prospects in sleepy little Globe, but at least I'd made a friend, which was more than I'd had back in L.A. People I was friendly with, sure, but no one to get together with and have lunch or a cup of coffee.

I sold some more things after that—crystals and oils and some books, even a few of the embroidered skirts from India I'd ordered to see if anyone would be interested in the kind of clothing you couldn't get at the local Walmart— and eventually, eight o'clock swung around and it was time to shut everything down. Josie asked if I wanted her to stay and help clean up, but as there wasn't that much to do, I thanked her but said that wasn't necessary.

Because everyone had been tidy and had disposed of their used cups and napkins and plates in the recycling bin I'd set out, there wasn't much for me to do except gather up the uneaten food and set it on the bottom step so I could take it upstairs and put it in the refrigerator when I was done locking up. A pause to transfer that night's earnings into the little pouch the local Wells Fargo had supplied, and I was just about ready to call it a night.

The bells on the door jingled, and I glanced up, thinking that maybe someone had left a personal belonging behind and had come to retrieve it. But that possibility didn't quite seem right, since I hadn't found anything as I was tidying the store.

Then my eyes met those of the man who'd just entered the shop, and my heart dropped to somewhere roughly around my feet.

"Hello, Selena," said Lucien Dumond.

5

Lucien's Luck

SINCE I ONLY STARED AT HIM IN SILENCE, MY mouth dry, he moved a little farther into the store, an unpleasant smile playing on his thin lips. I hadn't seen him for more than six months, and so maybe that was part of the reason he looked so horribly, terribly out of place in my pretty shop with the soothing deep blue on the walls and Hazel's intricately painted constellations on the ceiling. His shaved scalp gleamed under the glow of the sconces on the walls, and the silver Scorpio symbol he wore around his throat glittered with each step he took.

"Does this silence mean you're surprised to see me?"

"I—" *Get it together, Selena,* I scolded myself. *He's on your ground—ground you've purified and blessed and warded.*

Although honestly, I had to wonder how good those wards actually were, since they obviously hadn't been able to prevent Lucien from entering the store.

"What are you doing here, Lucien?" I asked, glad that I sounded brisk and no-nonsense, and not frightened at all. Then again, the bold tone in my voice was probably due to the glass of merlot I'd finished fifteen minutes earlier rather than any true courage on my part.

His smile only widened. "Why, I wanted to see you. I don't think that was very fair, the way you just up and left L.A. without telling anyone." A long pause, during which his deep-set eyes, half shadowed under his sparse brows, seemed to glitter with secret amusement. "Or rather, without telling anyone except your mother. Good thing she was so open to passing on what she knew."

"If you hurt her—" I began, fury and fear building in me in equal measures. My mother tended to trust everyone she met, which made her a perfect target for someone like Lucien Dumond.

He put his hands on his hips. As usual, he wore black from head to toe—a black button-up shirt, black jeans, black biker boots. Heavy silver rings shone from all his fingers, and tribal tattoos peeked out from under his rolled-up cuffs and on his neck where the open collar of his shirt revealed them. Even in L.A., he attracted attention, but in

Globe, he would stick out like a crow in a flock of canaries.

"Of course I didn't hurt her," he said, now sounding wounded. "Why would I hurt someone who was so willing to give me the information I needed? No, she told me that you wanted a change of scenery and had moved to Arizona. She didn't have your exact address—it seems you told her you'd give her that later on—but once I knew your destination, it wasn't that hard to determine exactly where you'd ended up."

I reflected that I needed to tell my mother not to go spilling my secrets to every random guy who called asking for information. Then I realized there wasn't much point in asking her to be careful. She'd agree and tell me she was sorry, and then she'd be right back at it again. I loved my mother, but sometimes her lack of caution drove me right up a wall.

"So, now you're here," I remarked, doing my best to sound bored and unconcerned. "Again I have to ask, what do you want?"

The expression of false affability he'd been wearing abruptly vanished. "You didn't ask permission to leave."

"I *what?*" I said, not sure I'd heard him correctly…or at least thinking that I couldn't have *possibly* heard him correctly. "Since when do I have to ask permission of you to do anything?"

His eyes narrowed, turning to slits. Tone silky, he replied, "As head of GLANG, I am in charge of all magical practitioners in the L.A. area. You're a magical practitioner, aren't you?"

"I'm a hedgewitch," I shot back, matching him glare for glare. "I don't work for anyone, I don't answer to anyone. Including you."

"How sweet that you think you have an opinion in the matter," he said, apparently not at all perturbed by the death stare I'd turned on him. That is, I hoped it was a death stare. Since more than once I'd been asked if I was the spokesmodel for a popular game show, I had a feeling that the borderline perky looks I'd inherited from my mother weren't doing me any favors. Maybe it had been a mistake to give myself bangs. "I am the strongest magical practitioner in the Los Angeles basin. That means I call the shots."

What a load of garbage. I wanted to tell Lucien that it didn't matter what kind of rules he made up in his diseased brain; I wasn't beholden to him…or to anyone else, for that matter.

Unfortunately, he was telling the truth about one thing. He was a much stronger magic worker than I could ever hope to be, partly because he didn't care if he cut corners or performed rituals that severely affected his karma.

And then there was the dirty little secret he'd been hiding from his followers and acolytes, something none of them had apparently picked up on but which I'd sensed the moment I met him.

Part of the reason he was so strong was that he used dark spells to tap into the powers of the people he kept around him. As far as I could tell, none of them had been able to sense what he was up to, but I'd felt it right away when we first crossed paths, had almost been able to see the energy moving from them into his body.

It was an incredible perversion of the craft, but I knew Lucien didn't give a damn about that. No, all he wanted was to draw more people to him, to surround himself with those who could feed the spells he created to keep his rich and powerful clientele happy. And if you got in the way of those spells, or did anything that might make someone think he wasn't quite on the up and up, then he had absolutely no compunction about squashing you like a bug.

I wasn't about to tell him that I'd learned what he was hiding, of course. The man was dangerous enough on his own; I didn't want to think how he'd react if he knew I'd discovered what he was up to.

Time to try a different tack. "I'd think you'd want to be rid of me, considering the way I poached that one client of yours."

Of course, I hadn't really poached her—she'd

come to me of her own volition—but I figured I wasn't above buttering up Lucien Dumond if it meant I could get him out of my life that much quicker.

His lips thinned almost to nonexistence. "Oh, but you cut her loose, so I suppose that transgression can be forgiven." A pause, and then the annoyance vanished from his face, and he smiled again, this time the open, friendly smile he probably used on his clients. For all I knew, it worked. The man wasn't attractive in a conventional way, but he did have a certain perverse charm. "And Selena, I never wanted to get rid of you. I wanted you to work with me…to *be* with me."

Personally, I would rather have gone to bed with a rattlesnake, but I knew I couldn't let my disgust show. I didn't know how I was going to get rid of him, and yet I all too clearly understood that informing him I would never be with him in the way he wanted was a recipe for disaster. Men like Lucien Dumond didn't like being told no.

"I'm not really a fan of being part of a harem," I said lightly. "Doesn't work with my lifestyle."

He shrugged. "I can get rid of all of them," he replied. A snap of his fingers, followed by, "Just like that."

"How very self-sacrificing," I said.

Once again, his eyes narrowed. "You're worth more than all of them put together. But if you combined your powers with mine…we could move worlds."

Was that a leer on his face? Judging by the way his gaze moved downward to take in the slight hint of cleavage my embroidered shirt revealed, I had to guess it probably was. Disgust curdled in my stomach, but once again, I told myself I had to play it cool.

"I'm not really interested in moving worlds," I told him, then stepped over to a display of crystal and gemstone spheres in various shapes and sizes and colors. After adjusting one minutely, I looked over my shoulder. He hadn't moved, but instead watched me with those gimlet eyes. "To be perfectly honest, I'd been thinking about getting out of L.A. for a while. This opportunity came up, so I took it. Maybe I should have let you know, but I didn't think it would be that big a deal."

"It is a big deal," he said. "A very big deal."

Great. Clearly, Lucien wasn't going to take any of my excuses as a reason to leave me alone. I found myself wishing that the store had one of those panic buttons under the counter, the kind they pushed at the bank to summon the cops when a robbery was in progress. Even if I'd had one, though, it wouldn't have summoned Calvin Standingbear, since he wasn't a member of the Globe P.D.

Too bad. It would have been amusing to

watch Calvin pound Lucien into the ground like a tent stake.

Not that he would have gotten that far, I realized soberly. Calvin probably had a good five inches and twenty pounds on Lucien, but he didn't have magic at his disposal, which made all the difference. Lucien could have drawn enough of Calvin's life force to make himself stronger and his opponent weaker, and Calvin would never be able to figure out why he hadn't been able to best someone he should have physically outmatched.

"Look," I replied, trying not to sound too desperate, "it's been a long day, and I'm tired. Why don't we meet for breakfast tomorrow and discuss this further then?"

For a moment, he didn't reply, only continued to survey me out of those narrowed eyes, as if he was trying to determine what kind of game I was playing. And really, I wasn't playing anything. I knew we'd only keep going back and forth over the same ground, and I was tired. Not that I thought meeting for breakfast would change anything, but, if nothing else, it would give me more time to think and formulate a plan.

Since the silence was growing uncomfortable, I added, "You are staying somewhere around here, aren't you?"

"Yes," he said shortly. "Athene and I got an Airbnb here in town."

Athene Kappas was Lucien's right-hand woman. I'd never been able to tell whether their relationship was sexual in nature or not, but she handled all his business and always appeared at his side. For all I knew, he'd made her be his chauffeur on this little Arizona road trip. I wouldn't put it past him.

In a way, I had to laugh at the gall of a man who would drive all the way from L.A. to Globe to importune me into being his partner while dragging his possible-paramour along for the ride. It seemed so inimitably Lucien.

But I only smiled sweetly and said, "Well, bring her along. I'm sure all three of us will have a lot to discuss."

He didn't take the bait, though. "No, I think it's better if you and I meet alone. Where?"

"The Flatiron," I said, naming a café where I'd had a couple of decent breakfasts since coming to town. "It's over on Highway 60."

"I'll find it," he replied. "Ten o'clock tomorrow."

"Ten o'clock," I repeated, glad that he hadn't suggested a time at the crack of dawn. But then, that sort of meeting would have been even more inconvenient for him than it would have been for me. I'd gotten the impression that the man was a complete night owl.

To my relief, he didn't push it after that, but

instead headed toward the door, which had been left slightly ajar after he entered. "Tomorrow," he said ominously, then swept out.

I didn't bother to respond, but only went over to the door and locked it behind him. That task done, I glanced around the store. Everything was in its place, everything as it should be, and yet I still felt as though something had gone seriously wrong with the world.

Well, I'd deal with all that the next day. For the time being, I was just going to head to bed and figure out tomorrow, tomorrow.

At least the store opening had gone well.

I put myself together decently the next morning, mostly because I planned to go straight to the shop after breakfast with Lucien. Well, unless he turned me into a toad or something. A few weeks earlier, I wouldn't have thought such a thing was even a possibility, but Archie's experience had taught me not to take anything for granted.

"Who was that man?" he asked, planting himself on his haunches in the entrance to the bathroom as I applied mascara.

"What man?" I responded.

Archie let out a soft hiss. "The man you were arguing with last night."

"You were eavesdropping?"

"Hardly," Archie said, now sounding bored. "I was sleeping on the landing, and your voices carried quite clearly up the staircase. You didn't sound very happy with him."

"That's because I wasn't," I said. Because I figured it couldn't hurt to give my resident cursed cat some background, I added, "He's—he's a sorcerer from L.A. He's also a world-class ass, and I'm less than thrilled that he tracked me down here. But done is done, so now I have to deal with it."

"And how are you going to 'deal with it'?"

"I'm meeting him for breakfast."

"That's supposed to solve everything?"

I slipped the tube of mascara back into my cosmetic case and pulled out my favorite MAC lipstick. Thank the Goddess that I could still mail-order the shades I knew and loved, although I was going to miss going into the store in person to try out new colors.

"Honestly, I don't know if it's going to solve anything," I said after I'd applied a light coating of Antique Velvet to my lips. "But I have to try. At least this way, there's a slim chance I'll be able to persuade him to let me stay here in Globe rather than haul me back to L.A."

At once, Archie's golden-green eyes slitted in

alarm. "You can't let him do that. I was just starting to get comfortable here."

I shook my head. "Yeah, Archie, it's all about you."

Being Archie, he didn't seem at all embarrassed that I'd called him out on his selfishness. Not for the first time, I wondered if he'd been the same way as a human, or whether his selfish streak had emerged over the decades while he was hustling to stay alive as an alley cat.

"It should always be about ourselves," he said, sounding huffy. "After all, who else can we trust to look out for our own best interests?"

For a second, I considered asking him whether he was a devotee of Ayn Rand, because his comment sounded exactly like that author's self-serving philosophies. But since I didn't want to get sidetracked, I decided to let the matter go.

"I'm going to try appealing to his better nature," I told the cat, even as I privately wondered whether Lucien Dumond had a better nature to appeal to. Still, I had to try. "Or at least, I'm going to do my best to persuade him that there's no reason why he'd even want me back in L.A. With any luck, I'll convince him that I'm a mediocre witch and no one he needs to waste his energy on."

"I'd be happy to help you with that argument," Archie said with a sniff. "Considering you've been here nearly three weeks and you still haven't turned me back into a human."

More than once during that time, I'd done my best to tell him I really wasn't that kind of a witch. Obviously, those words hadn't yet sunk in. I needed to save my arguing energy for dealing with Lucien, though, and so I just shrugged as I stowed my makeup bag back in its drawer. "I've been doing what research I can, Archie. There are only so many hours in the day. I did just put a store and an apartment together in three weeks, you know."

The cat made a harrumphing noise—coming from that throat, it sounded more like he was about to cough up a hairball—and stalked out of the bathroom.

Just as well. Although I was used to him hanging around while I put on my makeup, it was sometimes annoying to have to dodge questions while applying lipstick.

I went to the little hand-painted box on the dresser that held my jewelry and pulled out my favorite dangly amethyst earrings. The weather had started to warm up, so I wore a scoop-necked black T-shirt over my favorite purple and black sequined skirt, and black ballet flats instead of boots. It had always been one of my favorite outfits, and I hoped it would give me some courage for the coming confrontation.

Because I definitely wasn't getting dolled up just to impress Lucien Dumond. I had my planned lunch with Hazel as well. Good thing we'd decided to meet at one; that would give me plenty of time to get this breakfast with Lucien over with.

Ten minutes until ten. I grabbed my purse and hurried downstairs, then went out the back door into the alley. That was one drawback about my new home; it didn't have a garage or even a carport.

But Brett had helped me put up one of those canvas and steel car shelters, and that had helped to keep my poor Beetle from getting hopelessly dirty. Even so, I knew I'd need to take it to get washed pretty soon, since the shelter didn't keep all the dust out.

I knew I was preoccupying myself with silly concerns like the car because I didn't want to think about this face-to-face with Lucien. While I had to hope he wouldn't make too much of a scene in a public place—my entire reasoning for asking him to meet me at the Flatiron in the first place—I couldn't know that for sure. It was entirely possible he'd cause some sort of commotion embarrassing enough that I'd be forced to leave Globe just to avoid the fallout.

Or not, I told myself as I headed down Broad Street toward the restaurant. *What do you care what people think? You've already outed yourself as a witch, so who cares if Lucien starts haranguing you about your powers or whatever? This isn't high school.*

No, it wasn't, thank the Goddess. All the same, even a functioning adult generally wasn't thrilled at the prospect of creating a scene around the people they had to live and work with.

My nerves were fairly vibrating with anxiety by the time I pulled into The Flatiron's parking lot. I didn't see Lucien's car—a big black Mercedes S-Class sedan with California plates would have been pretty conspicuous amongst all the pickup trucks and SUVs—but I had a feeling he wanted to be late on purpose so he could make an entrance.

Whatever.

I touched the amulet of black tourmaline I carried in an inner pocket of my purse, hoping that its ability to absorb or even repel negative energy would be enough to protect me. Right after I'd gotten up that morning, I'd lit a protection candle and uttered an invocation to Cerridwen, goddess of the earth, that she might give me the strength I needed for this confrontation, but I still wasn't feeling all that confident. Ordinary people I could deal with…but Lucien Dumond was a whole order of magnitude beyond ordinary.

Since it was later in the morning, the restaurant wasn't too crowded. I managed a smile at Ingrid, the owner, who was doing hostess duty.

"Any place you like, Selena," she told me as she handed me a menu.

"Thanks," I replied. "Can I have another menu? A friend is meeting me."

Interest sparked in her light blue eyes. "'Friend'?" she echoed. "Anyone I know?"

I supposed at some point I'd get used to the casual nosiness of small-town dwellers. "No," I said, trying to sound casual. "A friend from L.A."

"Oh," she said, sounding a little disappointed. I couldn't be sure, but I was starting to get the feeling that a bunch of the local busybodies had started a pool to see how long it would take before I started dating someone.

Well, if that was the case, they were going to be waiting a long time. Not that I had anything against dating, per se, only that it hadn't worked out so well for me in the past. Over the last couple of years, I'd spent my energies focusing on the craft and my practice, since I'd gotten the distinct feeling that a happy love life was not something I was destined to enjoy during this particular lifetime. Maybe my dismal love life was merely karma…or maybe just really bad luck.

I took the menus over to a table that overlooked the parking lot, figuring at least that way I could see when Lucien pulled up and steel myself for his arrival at the table. No sign of the black Mercedes yet, though.

A waitress I didn't recognize—and who looked barely out of high school, if even that—came by and asked if I wanted anything to drink. Since I didn't know how long I'd be waiting for Lucien to appear, I asked for some hot water and a basket of herbal tea. It wasn't that I avoided caffeine altogether, but I was already on edge and didn't see the need to make myself even more jangly.

Ten o'clock came and went. My tea arrived, and I wasted some time in the ritual of choosing which variety I wanted from the little basket provided, then pouring hot water over the bag I'd selected. While I waited for it to cool down enough to drink, I got out my phone and frowned at the time stamp.

Ten fourteen.

Hmm. I didn't have any missed calls or texts, so it wasn't as though Lucien had tried to reach out and let me know he was running late. I supposed he could have gotten lost, although that wasn't such an easy thing to do in Globe, especially in a late-model Mercedes that I assumed had a top-of-the-line navigation system.

A big white SUV with some sort of logo on the door pulled into one of the empty parking spaces. I couldn't tell what was on the logo, since the vehicle was nearly pointed dead on toward the table where I sat. A minute later, the door opened, and Calvin Standingbear got out, black hair shimmering in the bright morning sun.

If possible, he was even more impressive in full daylight.

The logo on his SUV was probably the badge of the San Ramon tribal police department. I wondered what he was doing here, then thought he probably had stopped in to get a cup of coffee to go or something. After all, the restaurant was located right on Highway 60, and he could come and go from here more easily than heading over to Cloud Coffee, the coffee shop located just down the street from my loft and store.

I picked up my tea, extracted the bag, then blew on the hot liquid within the mug. The sharp, clean scent of peppermint drifted up to my nose, and I breathed it in. If nothing else, it would probably help calm me a bit.

The door to the restaurant opened, and Calvin walked in. He greeted Ingrid, but his eyes were already tracking to the various tables inside and their various occupants.

Until his gaze landed on me.

He walked over to the table, stride purposeful. At once, my heart started hammering away in my chest. What was he doing here? Had he decided that he'd blown it by not talking me up a bit more at the store opening? Was he at The Flatiron because he realized he wanted to ask me out on a date?

Even as I chided myself for allowing those ridiculous thoughts to churn away in my head, he came to a stop next to my table. For someone on a social call, he looked awfully grim.

"Selena Marx?" he said, voice brisker than it had been the night before. Actually, it was down-right abrupt.

"Hi, Calvin," I responded, hoping it was okay to address him by his first name. I knew if I tried to call him "Chief Standingbear," I'd sound like an idiot.

He didn't blink. Instead, he withdrew a piece of paper from his pocket, unfolded it, and slid it across the tabletop toward me. "Do you know this man?"

I looked down at the paper. On it was a fuzzy picture of Lucien Dumond, one that looked as though it had been enlarged from a driver's license. "Ye-es," I said, my voice shaky. Cold went over me, and as though from very far away, I heard the harsh squawk of a raven.

No, not from inside the restaurant, or even out in the parking lot. I knew it had come from much farther than that.

A harbinger.

"That's Lucien Dumond," I went on, since Calvin hadn't said anything else, only stood there, looming over my table. "He's visiting from Los Angeles."

Face still impassive, Calvin said, "His body was found early this morning." A pause before he added, "I'll need you to come with me."

6

Under Suspicion

I REALLY DIDN'T KNOW WHAT TO EXPECT FROM a tribal police station. Honestly, I'd never even been in a regular police station, so I had no frame of reference beyond what I'd seen on TV or in the movies.

The San Ramon tribal police headquarters were located in a newish building on the reservation, with what looked to be up-to-date computers and phones and office furniture. The glossy surroundings surprised me a little, since I hadn't expected anything quite so modern, not when Globe itself felt as if it was stuck somewhere back in the '80s…and that was being charitable.

To my relief, Calvin hadn't put me in handcuffs or anything. In fact, he'd allowed me to drive my car back to the apartment so I wouldn't have to leave it in the parking lot at The Flatiron. I'd tried to stammer to him that there must be some kind of mistake, that I hadn't seen Lucien since he left the store a little before nine the night before, but he didn't want to hear anything of it. He told me he'd take my statement at the police station, and instructed me to get in the back seat of his Dodge Durango.

And then we'd driven out to tribal lands.

Now we sat in Calvin's office. He'd left the door open, but everyone in the station seemed to have been instructed to stay away, since no one was working at either of the desks immediately outside.

He'd also been conscientious enough to get me a cup of water. I gulped from it and said, "I don't understand what's going on."

Expression sober, he replied, "Two of my people found Dumond's body dumped on a river-bank when they went to go fishing this morning. His wallet with I.D. was still on him—along with nearly five hundred dollars in cash. Obviously, robbery wasn't the motive. He's been taken to the county M.E. for an autopsy, but right now, best guess as to time of death was around midnight last night." Calvin's dark eyes narrowed, feeling like a pair of black laser beams as they focused on me. "Care to tell me where you were?"

"I was home in bed," I said. For the moment, I thought it better to stick to the facts. I couldn't really process my feelings about Lucien's death, especially since I thought I might be more relieved than anything else…or I would have been, if I weren't sitting in the San Ramon tribe's police station, getting grilled by the chief. "Where else would I have been? I was exhausted after the store opening."

Something flickered in Calvin's eyes. Was he remembering me at the store, how excited I'd been to have the place open and people actually coming in and buying things? Maybe he was trying to reconcile the woman he'd seen then with the kind of person who'd be able to murder a man in cold blood.

"Got anyone who can corroborate that?"

He probably knew perfectly well that I didn't. The whole town knew I lived alone. And all right, Archie had been there, had known I'd collapsed in bed a little after ten o'clock, but I kind of doubted the word of a talking cat was anything I could plausibly offer as support for my alibi.

"No," I said. I almost added that anyone in the area would have been able to see that I hadn't left the building after I locked up the store, but who would have even been around to notice? None of the other lofts in my particular block were used as residences, and while there was a small apartment building—formerly a dormitory for miners—at one end of the street, it was far enough away that I doubted the people who lived there would have seen any activity on my block. "But it's the truth." I hesitated, then added, "How —I mean—"

"How did it happen?" Calvin asked. "He was stabbed multiple times with a knife. We haven't found the murder weapon yet, so I can't tell you what type." He stopped there, arms folded over his chest. The sleeves of his khaki uniform shirt were rolled up, and I noticed for the first time that he had an interesting tattoo on the underside of one arm—the phases of the moon, waxing and waning against his smooth brown skin. "Do you own a knife, Ms. Marx?"

"Selena," I said automatically, even as a painful, worried lump began to form in my throat.

Because I did happen to own a knife. Several, actually. The athame, or goddess dagger, used in a variety of rituals, and the boline, a small, sharp blade used to cut up plants and papers and other items used in all sorts of ceremonies. The athame, because its purpose was purely ceremonial, didn't have a functioning point or blade, although I suppose if you shoved it into a person hard enough, it might penetrate the flesh. The boline was sharp enough along its edge, I supposed, but Calvin had said that Lucien had been stabbed, and the boline was definitely not a stabbing kind of knife.

I thought it was probably better to admit to owning them. After all, I had nothing to hide, right?

He repeated the question. "Do you own a knife…Selena?"

I lifted my eyes to meet his. "Yes, I do. They're ceremonial blades, used in spell-casting and other rituals. I'd be more than happy to show them to you."

His gaze held mine for a moment. Right then, I wished I knew him better so I'd know whether I saw anything to worry about in those cool dark eyes. But I didn't, so I just sat still and waited.

Then he said. "That's probably a good idea. Let's go back to your place."

Under other circumstances, I would have been thrilled to hear him utter those words. As it was, about all I could hope was that he'd take one look at the athame and the boline, and realize they weren't possibly sturdy enough to have struck down a man in his prime.

On the drive back to Globe, my brain kept working away at the problem. Part of me wondered how anyone could have gotten the drop on Lucien Dumond. After all, he was a sorcerer with a grab bag of pretty nasty tricks at his disposal. Besides that, though, he was also in good shape, did yoga and sparred with masters in a variety of martial arts. Even leaving magic out of it, he was not the sort of person who should have gone down easily.

But I didn't have all the details. Calvin hadn't told me very much, which I supposed made some sense. He wasn't going to let a possible perpetrator be privy to all the facts of the case.

When we drove down Broad Street, I glimpsed a couple of people paused by the front door to my store. They appeared to be staring at the "Be Back In..." sign, puzzled, probably wondering why it was almost noon and the place wasn't open.

Although I didn't say anything, Calvin seemed to notice, because he said, "This shouldn't take too long. Then you can go on with your day."

"I'm not under arrest?"

"Not yet."

As responses went, that wasn't exactly the most reassuring thing I could have heard. I shifted in my seat. "Why would you even think I was a suspect? There's no motive."

His jaw tightened, although he kept his gaze fixed on the street as he turned the corner so he could drive around back and park there. I supposed I should be glad that he wasn't going to march in the front door of the shop with me; this way, maybe no one would even notice that the chief of the tribal police had taken me for a little ride.

"There were reports that you and the victim were arguing last night," Calvin said. "According to Max Anders, it sounded pretty heated."

Irrational anger flared in me. Damn it. Had Lucien left the door to Blue Moon open on purpose so the neighbors could overhear our argument? I didn't even know why Max would have been hanging around his shop at that time of night, except I'd learned during the few weeks I'd been living in Globe that he tended to come and go at odd hours.

"So, we were arguing," I said coolly. "Lots of people argue. That doesn't mean someone's going to end up murdered."

"True," Calvin agreed as he parked the Durango next to the shelter covering my blue Beetle. "But it still establishes a motive. Want to tell me what the argument was about?"

I really didn't, for a variety of reasons. However, I guessed that holding back really wasn't an option. "Sure," I said. "After we get inside."

That request didn't seem to faze him; he nodded, and we got out of the SUV and went inside the building. After climbing the stairs to my apartment, we headed into the living room. He didn't seem inclined to sit down, but only leaned up against the mantel, arms folded as he waited for me to speak.

"Lucien has"—*had,* I thought, but decided not to stop—"a really successful practice as a spiritual adviser to a lot of Hollywood celebrities and other high-powered people. He'd been trying to get me to join his organization for almost two years."

"You're a spiritual adviser, too?" Calvin asked, now looking almost amused.

"I'm a witch," I said simply. "I wouldn't say that counseling people was all I did, but it was definitely part of it. I guess Lucien was angry that I left L.A. without consulting him. He was trying to talk me into going back."

For a few seconds, Calvin was silent, appearing to digest what I'd told him. "You had a personal relationship?"

"No," I replied at once, wanting to disabuse him of that particular disgusting notion as quickly as I could. *Not for lack of trying,* my brain told me, but I pushed the annoying inner voice aside. "It was just business…and barely that. Anyway, yes, we argued, but he left after agreeing to meet me for breakfast so we could talk once we'd had a chance to cool down a bit." Another thought struck me, and I added, "If I'd gone off and murdered him, why would I be sitting at The Flatiron, waiting for him to show up?"

"To make it look as though you were innocent," Calvin said in reasonable tones.

All right, he had me there. "Maybe," I allowed. "But that's not what happened. Anyway, let me show you my knives."

Without waiting to see if he was following—I knew he would—I led him down the hall to my office. That was where I'd set up my altar, since I really didn't have enough room in the master bedroom. The altar sat on a table opposite a computer desk, and was really just a green cloth embroidered with a tree and a border of leaves, my Tarot cards in their embroidered pouch, various crystals and vials of herbs, my leatherbound Book of Shadows, and a variety of bud vases filled with wildflowers I'd collected from various spots around town.

Off to one side lay the athame and the boline. I pointed at them, saying, "Those are my knives. They're used for rituals, nothing else."

Calvin approached the altar, dark eyes alight with curiosity. And although he leaned down to take a closer look, I noticed right away that he was careful not to touch anything. "It's very nice," he said, sounding almost surprised.

Stupidly, I had to fight to prevent a pleased smile from spreading across my lips. I'd worked very hard to assemble items that were both meaningful and beautiful, that fulfilled both form and function. That he'd noticed made an absurd sort of happiness spread through me.

But we were there on much darker business. "Do you need to take them into evidence?" I asked.

"I should," he replied. "Is that going to be a problem?"

Well, it would, just because I needed those items for my rituals. But I had a feeling that protesting would only make me sound guilty, so I shrugged. "Not really. I mean, I can manage without them for a while."

I almost added that I had several more athames and bolines down in the store and therefore could borrow some of them if push came to shove…then figured it was probably better for me to keep my mouth shut on that particular subject. The last thing I wanted was for him to think I had a whole shop full of murder weapons just waiting to be used.

"It shouldn't be too long," he told me as he extracted a pair of latex gloves and a clear plastic bag from his pocket. After sliding on the gloves, he picked the knives up one by one and deposited them in the baggie, then zipped it shut. "I just need the lab to go over them."

Although having the knives spirited away for inspection would be an inconvenience, I wasn't too worried about anything the lab would find.

After all, I knew I hadn't stabbed Lucien Dumond, and so the most incriminating evidence a crime lab might find on the blade would be paper fibers and maybe a bit of wax residue from spatter when I blew out the altar candles.

"Have you talked to Athene?" I asked next, thinking it couldn't hurt to move suspicion to a more likely target.

"'Athene'?" Calvin repeated with a frown as he pulled off the gloves and stowed them in a pocket of his trousers.

Of course, he wouldn't have known about her. It wasn't as if Lucien probably had anything on his person that connected him to the woman who helped with the day-to-day business of GLANG. In fact, Calvin probably didn't know about the Airbnb, either. The gossip mill in Globe was pretty efficient, but I assumed even it had its limits…especially since the town's biggest rumor-monger—i.e., Josie Woodrow—had probably been distracted by my store opening.

"She's Lucien's business partner," I said. "He told me they'd come to town together."

"Were they close?"

I had a feeling he'd asked that question because he wanted to know if there might have been some component of jealousy involved in Lucien's murder. Maybe there was. Athene had seemed cool and in control the few times I'd met her, but that didn't necessarily mean anything. Sometimes a cool exterior hid a raging volcano.

"Do you mean, were they romantically involved?"

He nodded. "Some might say there was sufficient motive if they had a relationship and he'd brought her with him to coax another woman back to Los Angeles."

When you put it that way....

"I suppose so," I allowed. "But honestly, I don't know for sure. Lucien always had a lot of women around him."

"Romantic partners?"

"I think using the term 'romantic' isn't exactly accurate." I paused then, wondering how much I should tell Calvin Standingbear. Then again, the more information I supplied that could point the finger of suspicion away from me, the better. Hands planted on my hips to give me some reassurance, I went on, "I guess a lot depends on how much you're willing to believe."

The straight, dark bars of his brows lifted slightly. "Believe about what?"

"About Lucien's powers."

"'Powers,'" Calvin repeated.

I nodded, then waited. No point in me trying to convince him of something he didn't want to accept as real. Some people were willing to have an open mind, and some weren't.

After a brief pause, he said, "Let's just say I've seen enough in this world to convince me there are some things that can't be explained."

If I'd been holding my breath, I would've let out in a relieved gust right then. As it was, I could only thank the universe that Calvin wasn't close-minded the way so many other people were. And honestly, I got it. I'd had enough evidence early on to support the belief that the ordinary, day-to-day world most people lived was overlaid by a world of esoteric powers and forces, of entities that had nothing to do with our mundane lives.

Some people never pierced that veil, though, and so it was almost impossible to convince them of anything that wasn't right in front of their eyes.

I uttered a silent thank-you to the universe that apparently Calvin Standingbear wasn't one of them.

"Well, then," I said. "I don't know exactly how he did it, because I don't mess around with those sorts of dark spells, but from what I could tell, he had the ability to draw energy from the people around him. Whatever gifts they possessed—and he always made sure to find people who had some form of psychic ability, even if it wasn't very strong—he drew it out of them to power his enchantments. And one of the most efficient ways of drawing that power from them was through sex magic."

Those two words fell like a thud in the middle of the conversation. For a long moment, Calvin just stared at me, dark eyes speculative. Was he wondering if I'd practiced that sort of magic? I hadn't, because I had my own ways of focusing my energies, but just the idea that he might be imagining me engaged in that kind of ritual made hot blood rush to my cheeks.

"So, that's what he practiced?" Calvin asked next.

Once again, I had to thank the universe that this time he hadn't asked for any sort of elaboration on what that kind of magic actually entailed.

I nodded. "Among other things. But anyway, that's why Lucien always had a lot of women around him. I only saw him with Athene a couple of times, and I didn't see anything in their interactions that hinted they were intimate, but I can't say for sure."

"Do you know where I can find this Athene?"

"Athene Kappas," I said, figuring he should have her full name. "Lucien told me they'd rented an Airbnb somewhere around here, but he didn't give me any details."

"That's all right," Calvin replied. "There are only a couple here in Globe. I'll contact each of the owners and see if Athene is staying there."

Although I'd never warmed up to Athene— her chilly personality and utter devotion to Lucien precluded any kind of friendly connection between us—I couldn't quite hold back the burst of pity I felt at the thought of her sitting alone in that Airbnb, waiting for Lucien to return. I assumed he must have told her that he was meeting me for breakfast, and so, even though it was now past one o'clock in the afternoon, maybe she still hadn't begun to suspect anything. Maybe she was sitting there, looking at the time on her phone and worrying that her partner's extended absence had to mean he'd been successful, and he and I had gone off together somewhere. It was just the sort of maneuver Lucien would pull...if he was still alive, of course.

Or she could have packed her bags and headed out of town once she'd made sure he was dead. Either possibility seemed equally plausible.

"Did you find his car key?" I asked.

"Mercedes?" he responded, and I nodded. "The fob was in his pocket, along with his wallet. Like I said, robbery didn't seem to be the motivation."

There went that theory. I didn't see how Athene could get out of town if she didn't have the key to Lucien's car. Unless they'd come here in separate vehicles, but that scenario seemed a little far-fetched. He wouldn't have wanted to give up the opportunity to have a captive audience during the nearly eight-hour drive from L.A.

"Well, I hope you can find her," I said.

"I do, too," he responded. "I'm hoping she can give me some answers. In the meantime, I'd like you to stick around."

The request didn't surprise me too much. I managed a wan smile. "I just opened a store. Where would I go?"

To my surprise, he offered me an answering grin. "Just covering my bases, Selena. I'll let myself out."

With a nod, he headed out of my office and down the hall to the apartment's front door. A moment later, it closed quietly behind him.

Absurdly, I wished I could have thought of a reason to make him stay. Offered him lunch or something. Which I knew was beyond silly. The guy was conducting a murder investigation.

And, for the moment, I was the prime suspect.

Doing my best not to sigh, I got out my phone and called Hazel. It was already past time for our lunch date, and for all I knew, she'd already found out what had happened to Lucien, but I wouldn't leave her hanging.

Life had never been this complicated in L.A.

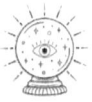

7

River Adventures

"OH, MY *GOD!*" SAID JOSIE AS SHE SAILED into the store, the watercolor-patterned scarf in tones of fuchsia and turquoise she had draped around her neck fluttering dramatically behind her. "I just *heard.*"

Just now? I thought. *It's been almost an hour since Calvin left. I thought you worked faster than that.*

Somehow, though, I managed to give a philosophical shrug. "It's crazy, isn't it? I mean, I can see why the police would want to talk to me, but I didn't have much to tell them."

She paused in front of the display case next to the cash register, hands planted on her substantial hips. "I went and told Calvin what an upstanding citizen you were, but he only said that he wasn't at liberty to discuss an open investigation." Her brilliant blue eyes fastened on me, concerned...but also curious. I knew she wanted to get the inside scoop.

Since I wasn't with the police, I didn't have any such barriers to communication.

"I was home the whole night," I went on. "You know how worn out I was from getting the store ready to open."

"Yes, of course," she said, now sounding almost impatient. "But do you have any idea who might have been involved?"

"I told Calvin to talk to Athene, Lucien's business partner."

"Yes, the woman who came to town with him yesterday," Josie responded, and I looked at her, startled. Before I could ask how she'd known that, she went on, "Oh, my friend Betsy rented them the house they were staying in. She inherited it from her mother, and instead of selling it, she fixed it up as a nice little vacation rental. Actually, she asked me to help with some of the decorating, and of course, I said yes. We got the cutest—"

"So, Lucien and Athene rented your friend's house," I cut in, knowing I needed to head Josie off at the pass if I didn't want to get an intimate recounting of every stick of furniture that had gone into the Airbnb in question.

"Yes," Josie said. She was probably so used to people interrupting her like that, she hadn't even noticed. "She said she wished she hadn't, because the neighbors had called to complain about the noise."

"The noise?"

"Apparently, they were playing some kind of very loud tribal-sounding music. It went on for at least an hour. Betsy was just about to go over there —even though it was almost midnight by that point—when it finally stopped and the neighbors saw somebody drive off in a big black car."

"Lucien's Mercedes," I murmured, and she tilted her head, eyes bright with interest.

"He had money?"

"Quite a bit, I think," I said. I sounded distracted even to myself, though, because my mind had already begun to race, trying to put the pieces together. So, Lucien had been at the house until nearly midnight. My best guess about the music was that he and Athene had been using it for some sort of ritual. What kind of ritual, I didn't know, although I had an uneasy feeling that they'd blasted the music to cover up the sound of some sort of sex ceremony.

For what purpose, though? To bind their powers together to create a spell that would compel me to follow him back to Los Angeles? I supposed that was possible, even while I didn't want to think that Athene would voluntarily participate in such an enchantment. Or maybe she honestly didn't care because she had no emotional attachment to Lucien at all. In that case, I guessed it was plausible that she'd go along with the scheme if it meant even greater success for GLANG in the long run.

"Have they found his car?" I asked, and Josie frowned.

"I honestly don't know," she replied. "As I said, Calvin wasn't exactly forthcoming, although this sort of thing affects all of us. Do you have any idea what a murder does to property values? Part of Globe's appeal is its public safety record."

Trust Josie to be concerned about that particular detail. Part of me wanted to be horrified at her lack of compassion for a crime victim, but then, she hadn't known Lucien. It made sense for her to focus on an aspect of the crime that would affect the town she loved so much.

"It sounded like they found Lucien somewhere on the reservation," I told her. "So, it's not exactly Globe that would be affected."

Her expression brightened a little. "Oh, well, if that's the case...." The words trailed off, and she focused back on me, now looking concerned. "Are you all right, Selena? This Lucien was a friend of yours, wasn't he?"

"I think 'friend' is stretching it a bit far," I replied. "We knew each other, but I wouldn't say we were friendly. It was more a business relationship than anything else…if you could even call it that."

"Well, it's still shocking. But I'm sure Calvin will get to the bottom of it soon enough. He's a very smart man, although this is the first time he's had to solve a murder."

Those words did nothing to relieve the worry that had tensed up the muscles in my neck and shoulders. I mean, it was one thing to know you were innocent. But when the circumstantial evidence pointed in your direction…evidence that would be analyzed by an inexperienced country police chief…well, let's just say it wasn't exactly confidence inspiring.

Still, I had to trust that my innocence would be proven once more evidence came to light. I didn't have any idea what Athene had told Calvin —if he'd spoken to her at all. Maybe she knew exactly what had happened to Lucien, and she'd bugged out before the authorities could catch up with her. The lack of a vehicle might not have been as big an impediment as I thought. Globe had one guy—Travis Cox—who drove for both Uber and Lyft…when he felt like it. Although I'd never availed myself of his services, since I had my own wheels, he'd dropped into the store a few times to buy some incense…probably in a vain attempt to hide the scent of marijuana that seemed to perpetually hang around him. What if

Athene had contacted Travis via her app and let him know that if he drove her to Mesa…or maybe all the way to Phoenix International Airport… she'd make it worth his while?

All right, I knew I was manufacturing worst-case scenarios. But considering Lucien Dumond had turned up dead within twelve hours of his arrival in Globe, I didn't think conjuring thoughts of gloom and doom was all that out of line.

"Yes, he seems very capable." And that was all I felt safe to say about Calvin Standingbear. The guy definitely had an overwhelming physical presence…one I couldn't seem to stop thinking about.

However, it seemed that Josie had picked up something in my tone, even though I'd tried my best to sound completely neutral. Her eyes twinkled, and she said, "Maybe he'll need to question you again."

"I doubt it," I replied quickly. Better to nip any speculation in the bud as fast as possible. "I really didn't have much to tell him."

The door to the shop opened, and a couple who looked like they were probably in their late fifties or early sixties walked in. Motorcycle enthusiasts, I guessed, judging by the bandanna that covered the man's gray ponytail and the leather jacket the woman wore over her "Durango, Colorado" T-shirt.

I'd never seen either of them before, and

guessed they must be tourists. And thank the Goddess for that—if they were just passing through Globe on their way to Phoenix…or maybe to Payson, depending on which way they were traveling…then they couldn't have heard anything about Lucien Dumond's murder, and couldn't possibly know that the owner of the quaint store where they were shopping was one of the prime suspects in the case.

Josie could clearly see that their arrival meant an end to our conversation. A look of disappointment passed over her face, but then she smiled and said, "I'll check back in later. I'm sure everything is going to be fine."

I had to hope she was right.

The biker couple bought some jewelry and a couple of books on crystals, so I had more than one reason to be glad they'd dropped in. After they left, my stomach growled, reminding me I hadn't eaten anything so far that day. Events had tumbled along ever since the moment Calvin Standingbear had turned up so unexpectedly at The Flatiron, but now my body was letting me know that, murder investigations notwithstanding, it needed to eat.

A sandwich from Cloud Coffee was probably

my best bet, but I hesitated, wondering whether it was a good idea to show my face in public like that when I'd just been taken away for questioning in a murder investigation. Then again, *I* knew I was innocent. If I began acting like I wasn't, then people would start looking at me as though I had to be guilty.

Also, my cupboards were nearly bare. I needed to do another shopping run, but getting ready for the store opening had kept me busy day and night.

You can do this, I told myself as I got my purse out from under the counter. *Just act natural.*

Sure.

I set the little "Be Back At" sign in the window to two o'clock, then locked the shop door. Cloud Coffee was only two blocks down and across the street from my store, so it didn't take me very long to get there. Since it was past one-thirty, the lunch crowd had mostly come and gone, although a couple of people lingered at tables with their laptops.

Bryan looked a little surprised to see me, although he recovered quickly enough, sending me a smile that seemed almost genuine. "Hi, Selena. What can I get you?"

"A chicken salad wrap and a decaf iced green tea," I replied. Their chicken salad was legendary. Also, it was the sort of thing that I could eat back at the store without worrying about making a mess.

"Coming right up."

I didn't see Bryan's husband Kris anywhere, but maybe he'd gone off to run an errand or something, since clearly, the lunch rush had ended. None of the people preoccupied with their laptops seemed to pay any attention to me, which had to be a good thing. Maybe Josie knew exactly what was going on, but she was the nexus of Globe's gossip circuit. Otherwise, it didn't seem as if the news had made the rounds yet.

Well, except for Bryan's odd reaction when I walked in. I had a feeling he'd heard something, or maybe Josie had stopped in for yet another latte on the way back to her office and had filled him in. I preferred to think that he'd heard the story directly from her, because at least that way, I could let myself believe not too many people knew about Lucien's murder.

As Bryan handed me the bag with my sandwich, I got a quick flash of his aura—its usual smoky blue, but with little sparks of orange and red around the edges. That could have been edginess from being in such close proximity to a murder suspect…or it could have been something else completely. My ability to see auras came and went, although if I concentrated hard enough, I could sometimes view them at will. For me to catch a glimpse like that when I wasn't even trying meant whatever emotion he was feeling, it was strong enough for me to pick up.

I just wished I knew what it was. Unfortunately, my psychic abilities didn't extend to mind reading.

I thanked him and headed back to Blue Moon. For the first time, I realized it really was a gorgeous day, the sun warm but the breeze cool, little white clouds chasing each other across the sky like a flock of celestial sheep.

The sort of day I'd hoped I might encounter after moving to such an out-of-the-way spot. It seemed a shame to waste it indoors.

The store just opened last night, I told myself with a mental shake. *You can't turn around and close it for the rest of the day just because the weather is nice.*

True. And it was a Saturday, and therefore my best chance at getting some tourist traffic. It was one thing to close the place down for twenty minutes so I could run out and grab a sandwich. It was something else entirely to shut it because I was getting spring fever.

Still, even though I went back to Once in a Blue Moon and dutifully took down the "Be Back At" sign—and hid my half-eaten chicken salad wrap under the counter when a few tourists actually did wander in—I couldn't quite ignore my itchy feet. Something was telling me I needed to get out.

Okay, then. I'd stay open for a while longer, but close early. Not too early, but early enough there would still be some daylight.

Daylight for what?

I got a quick flash in my mind—a fast-moving creek with grasses hanging over its bank, and the lush, fresh green of cottonwood trees in the background. A blink, and the image was gone.

Even as the question began to form in my mind, I realized what I'd seen.

The place where Lucien Dumond had died.

Oh, hell no, I told myself. *Bad enough you're a suspect. Now you want to go and disturb a crime scene?*

If there was even anything left to disturb. Surely, Calvin and his deputies had already gone over the spot with the police equivalent of a fine-tooth comb. Maybe I could go out there and poke around, see if I picked up on any vibes or got any psychic flashes. That happened to me sometimes as well; it wasn't all Tarot cards and pendulums and crystal balls.

And usually, if I was vibing with something, that meant I needed to follow my instincts.

At four-thirty, I put the sign back in the window, signaling that the store would be open again on Monday at 11 a.m. Since I'd noticed that most of the other locally owned shops in town had haphazard hours at best, I figured no one would mind too much if I wasn't open from ten to six every day. And although I still didn't quite know what I'd do with my days off, I figured I couldn't work seven days a week.

When I went upstairs, Archie lay in the middle of the hallway, licking a forepaw. His location had probably been chosen to ensure I couldn't possibly avoid him, so I stopped a few feet away and crossed my arms.

"It's too early for your dinner," I said.

Immediately, he stopped ministering to his paw and got to his feet. "So, now you're a murder suspect?"

Archie had made himself scarce during Calvin's visit—he definitely hadn't been loitering in the office, his usual hideout—but I realized it was too much to hope for that he'd slept through the whole thing. I gave what I hoped was a casual shrug as I said, "Maybe. I don't think Chief Standingbear knows what to make of the situation. He's pursuing another lead right now."

There, I'd managed to say his official name without cracking a smile.

However, my feline roommate didn't look impressed. "He came here to collect evidence."

"*Possible* evidence," I corrected him. "Anyway, I'm innocent, so there's nothing to worry about.

Actually, I'd think you'd be happy to know that Lucien is no longer a threat. At least you don't have to worry about me disappearing off to L.A."

"No, just to prison," Archie remarked, his tone lugubrious in the extreme. "For a witch, you don't seem to be very skilled at managing your own luck."

I wanted to tell him he didn't know what he was talking about, but since I had to admit that the last twenty-four hours hadn't been exactly all that great, I decided to keep from clapping back at the cat. "Working on it," I said. "In fact, I have something I want to check on before it gets dark, and we're burning daylight."

"Check on what?" he asked, green-gold eyes narrowing in suspicion as he followed me into the bedroom.

"I don't know yet."

Because I was already wearing a black T-shirt, I only had to slip out of my skirt and into a pair of jeans to prepare for my outing. As soon as my fingers slid beneath the elastic waistband of the sparkly peasant skirt, Archie's eyes widened in alarm, and he bolted from the room.

There. I knew that would work. Any time there was the slightest chance he'd see me anything but fully clothed, he beat a hasty retreat.

There was more than one way to manage a cursed cat.

When I emerged from the bedroom in jeans and hiking boots, he watched me with narrowed eyes. "I assume from the footwear that you're not going to Walmart."

"I might be," I allowed, since I thought I probably should head over to the store after I was done with my...well, whatever it was I intended to find out on the San Ramon Apache reservation.

For a second or two, the cat didn't respond. Then he let out a small huff and said, "I need more treats," before stalking into the office so he could curl up on his bed.

He really didn't—I made sure to keep a backup box of treats at all times—but I knew that was just his way of getting in the last word.

But at least I didn't have to waste any more time standing there and arguing with him. I grabbed my purse and let myself out of the apartment before hurrying down the back stairs.

I honestly didn't know where I was going. Or rather, I knew I needed to head out of town on Highway 70, going east, to get to San Ramon, the main settlement on the reservation, but what I'd seen in that flash of a vision had been a river, not a town. I sat in the car for a minute, scanning the map I'd brought up, locating the San Ramon River, which flowed just to the east of the town itself. The water in the vision hadn't looked wide enough to be a river, but I was starting to learn that "river" didn't necessarily mean the same thing in Arizona that it did in other places.

There also appeared to be lots of creeks and tributaries of the San Ramon, and maybe Lucien had been found next to one of them. Calvin had said his body had been found on a riverbank, but that didn't necessarily mean anything.

Just to be safe, I'd brought along one of my pendulums, the banded fluorite one that had always seemed the most helpful when it came to sharpening focus. Since I had to let the universe guide me to the right spot, I figured I could use all the help I could get.

And because the sun was already starting to sink toward the west, I knew I needed to get going.

About five minutes outside Globe, I passed Apache Gold, the casino the San Ramon tribe operated. I'd come this way before, of course, but this time I paid more attention to the structure, to how tidy and prosperous everything looked. The parking lot appeared pretty full, too. True, it was a Saturday afternoon, probably peak play time for any local gamblers, but still. No wonder the police station was so nice; the tribe probably had casino profits to burn.

I turned off the same place Calvin had when we'd gone to the station, figuring that driving through what counted as "downtown" San Ramon was just as good a route as anything else. The town—not much more than a collection of small houses and buildings that made Globe look like a bustling metropolis—passed by the car windows, quiet, unassuming. A lot of the houses looked like they were actually mobile homes, but everything appeared to be in good repair, the yards neatly kept.

Then I saw a sign that said "River Access" and turned right, following the narrow street until it came to an abrupt halt at a community parking lot. A white pickup truck was parked at the far end of the lot, but otherwise it seemed unoccupied.

End of the road. I pulled into one of the numerous empty spaces, then got out of the car. Hiking around on what could prove to be treacherous terrain while hauling my purse with me didn't seem like a very good idea, so I extracted my I.D., key fob, pendulum, and phone and shoved them into my pockets, then stowed the purse in the trunk and locked it.

Now mostly unencumbered, I followed the signs pointing me to the trailhead and began to walk. Already I heard the sound of water rushing a few yards away, while the long row of cottonwoods would have showed me exactly where the river was located even without the signage.

As I walked, I wondered how Lucien had

ended up here. Had he been murdered somewhere else? Had the killer brought his body here to dump it in the river, thinking that was the best way to get rid of it?

That made some sense...especially if the murderer was someone unfamiliar with the area, someone who couldn't have known that the currents would carry a body onto the bank rather than safely downstream.

Or maybe Lucien had come here under his own power. I remembered he was a Scorpio— double Scorpio, actually, with both his sun and ascendant in that powerful, mysterious water sign —and I supposed it was also possible that he'd come here to commune with the flowing water and try to tap into its energies. His house in Encino had fountains everywhere—in the court- yard, in the foyer, in almost every room.

But even if he'd come to the San Ramon River to blend its energies with his, someone must have followed him with evil in their heart. If he'd died from drowning, then I could have chalked up his death to a fatal accident and nothing more, but you didn't drown from multiple stab wounds to the chest. Or at least, even if it turned out that the actual cause of death was water in the lungs, he probably could have survived falling in the river if it weren't for that whole stabbing thing.

Since I seemed to be alone for the moment, I

pulled the fluorite pendulum from my pocket and paused on the path, letting it dangle in front of me. A second or two passed as it swung idly from side to side with no real pattern to its movements...until it appeared to almost reverse itself, tracing an arc that moved from me to the path ahead and then back again. In fact, it felt as if it had come alive, was pulling me in that direction.

Well, I'd come here for an answer from the universe. I supposed I'd better see what it wanted.

I moved forward as the sound of the water grew louder and louder. The path, to my relief, was fairly well marked and not too rocky, telling me this same route had been used by many people before me. A few yards more, and I reached the river bank.

The San Ramon was bigger than I'd expected, maybe around five yards from bank to bank. It moved briskly, too, chattering over rounded granite stones as it flowed to the southeast. Where all that water was coming from, I didn't know for sure, although I vaguely recalled that there were large mountain ranges to the north, places that might add their snow melt to the river in front of me.

Growing up in Southern California as I had, flowing water always fascinated me. Sure, I was used to the ocean, but the only time I'd ever seen an honest-to-goodness river was when I'd made a trip up to Big Bear years earlier.

The pendulum swung from my hand, pulling me toward the south. I did my best to follow, glad of my hiking boots, which I'd bought a couple of years earlier with the conviction that I was going to get up at the crack of dawn every day and hike Runyon Canyon in the Hollywood Hills. That particular resolution hadn't lasted very long, but at least I'd had the foresight to hang on to the boots instead of donating them the way I'd done with so many of my other belongings.

Despite the boots, I had to occasionally move slowly to maintain my footing. The cottonwood trees on either side of the water provided shade, but I realized it had been silly to come running out here without a bottle of water. Yes, there was the river, although I had a city girl's wariness of drinking anything that hadn't been filtered a hundred times. Who knew what might be living in there?

I shook my head at myself and trudged on. The pendulum still tugged at my hand, pulling me toward the south. I knew I needed to keep following it, even though I was already starting to feel as if this had been a crazy errand. What was I expecting to find? I knew that Calvin Standingbear's team wouldn't have left any evidence behind.

Physical evidence, I reminded myself. In places where people died violently, psychic residue often lingered. I hoped I'd be able to sense it, to get some kind of a read from those energies, even though I wasn't technically a medium and didn't have any real experience speaking with the dead.

About twenty yards down, the rocky bank smoothed itself into a stretch of coarse sand, almost like a miniature beach. Almost at once, I noticed footprints in that sand, and my heartbeat sped up a little. Was this where Lucien had been killed?

But even though I wasn't a forensics expert, I could tell right away that the prints were of various sizes, and crisscrossed the miniature beach before heading into the stand of cottonwood trees that sheltered the spot. I guessed they must have been left behind by Calvin and his team, or maybe some locals who'd come here to fish. He'd said that was who found the body, after all—a couple of local men whose fishing plans probably hadn't included walking onto a murder scene.

I didn't have time to be disappointed, though. As I took another step onto the little beach, a stab of fear went through me like the proverbial knife. I stood stock still, body thrumming with flight-or-fight responses, even as I told myself it was all right, that I was alone and nothing could hurt me here.

Pain and shock and fear. They reverberated all around the spot, and I realized this truly was where Lucien had met his end, even if these footprints might not be his, even if his body was now miles away at the local medical examiner's office.

I swallowed, and began to wonder whether this had been such a good idea after all. Despite my inner reassurances, I honestly didn't know whether I was all that safe. What if Lucien's vengeful ghost lingered in this place, just waiting for a chance to strike out at any hapless passersby?

But I wasn't just any stranger, blundering onto this spot. We'd known each other in life, and if there was even a chance he'd begun to haunt the scene of his death, I needed to try to reach out to him.

"Lucien?" I ventured, hating how shaky my voice sounded. *There's no reason to be afraid,* I told myself. *Ghosts can scare you, but they can't hurt you.*

At least, that was the standard party line when it came to the spirits of the departed.

No response. The air seemed heavier than it should be, laden with a memory of the violence that had happened in the secluded little spot.

The pendulum hung straight down from my hand, unmoving. That had to be a good sign, didn't it? If there was any evil spirit activity nearby, wouldn't it have been swinging wildly, telling me to get the hell out of there?

Maybe…or maybe not. I'd never been in this particular situation before…and neither had my pendulum.

Better to try again. "Lucien?" I asked.

A breeze fluttered by my cheek. It could have been just a bit of late afternoon wind, nothing supernatural at all.

Or maybe not.

The wind picked up, tugging at my loose hair. A few dark strands blew past my cheek, and I pushed them back with the hand that wasn't holding the pendulum.

The breeze seemed to be moving toward the water. Was there something in the river itself, something Calvin's team had overlooked?

I guessed I needed to find out.

The ground got rockier again at the water's edge. Gingerly, I made my way over the river stones, moving a few feet away from the bank. My boots were halfway submerged, but I'd splurged for the waterproof versions and had to hope they'd live up to their manufacturer's promises.

Wait—was that a glint of something metallic wedged down between the rocks?

I leaned down, squinting as I tried to make out the shape of the object between the mossy stones. Closer…closer….

"Hey!" came a man's voice, and I startled.

I caught a quick glimpse of Calvin Standing-bear striding toward the water, brows drawn together in annoyance. And that was the only glimpse I got, because as soon as I glanced back at him, I promptly lost my precarious balance and went ass over teakettle into the water.

My day just kept getting better and better.

8

Tea and Sympathy

"Just what the hell did you think you were doing?" Calvin asked.

At least he'd waited until I staggered out of the water, jeans dripping, before he started the interrogation.

"Looking around," I replied. I'd already figured there wasn't much point in trying to cover up what I'd been doing, so I thought it was better to tell the truth. "I was hoping I could pick up on any vibes that might help point me toward Lucien's murderer."

"'Vibes,'" Calvin repeated, expression still irritated. Then his eyes narrowed slightly. "How did you know this was the place where he was killed?"

Despite everything—and despite my waterlogged clothes and boots—I couldn't quite hold back an inner rush of triumph. So, my pendulum had led me to the right spot. "My pendulum," I answered.

That reply didn't seem to have mollified him. "Your what?" he asked.

I reached into my damp pocket and pulled out the object in question. Thank the Goddess I'd stowed it there before venturing out onto those precarious stones, or I might have lost it when I got dunked. Whether my phone and key fob had survived their immersion was something I'd have to wait to discover. "It's generally used for divination," I explained. "But I thought it might help as a guide for other things…and it looks like I was right."

Calvin appeared nonplussed. "You shouldn't be poking around out here. There are snakes and bobcats and coyotes. Bears and mountain lions sometimes, too."

"I thought the snakes hadn't started to wake up yet," I said innocently. "I read somewhere that it's still too cold overnight for them."

"That still leaves the bears and the bobcats and the coyotes…and the mountain lions. And that's leaving out contaminating a crime scene."

"Was I, though?" I asked. I didn't know whether I liked this gruff, official version of him, although I suppose he had every right to be annoyed with me. "It looks to me like you got everything cleared up pretty efficiently."

It wasn't intended as a compliment; I was only telling him the truth. Still, his expression softened just a bit. "My deputies and I went over the area, true." He seemed to take in my dripping clothes for the first time and added, "You need to get out of those wet things. My house is only about five minutes away—I can take you over there to get dried off."

Under most circumstances, I would've been overjoyed to get an invitation to Calvin Standingbear's house. As it was, I could tell he'd only decided to take pity on me, nothing more.

Still, I wasn't about to turn down his offer.

"My car is parked over in the lot—" I began, thinking I should offer some kind of token protest, but he shook his head.

"It'll be fine. You can come back and get it when you're ready." A twinkle entered those dark eyes as he went on, "I'll make sure no one writes you a ticket."

Those words seemed to seal the deal. "Okay."

I squelched along behind him as he led me through the trees and to a rough forest road a hundred yards or so away from the river. His white Durango waited there, and I climbed into the passenger seat after he opened the door for me.

Thank goodness the seats were leather. If they'd been cloth, they would have been as soaked as I was.

We rattled our way down the forest service road for a minute. To my surprise, we seemed to be heading deeper into the wilderness, rather than driving back out to the small lane that serviced the river recreation area.

Maybe I lifted my eyebrows or something. Whatever the reason for his response, Calvin said, "My place is kind of out in the middle of nowhere. Off-grid."

That sort of setup seemed more plausible out in the wilds of southeastern Arizona than it would have back in Southern California. "What if there's an emergency and someone needs to reach you?"

A faint smile touched his lips. "CB radio and satellite phone. And satellite for internet."

Well, at least it didn't sound as if he was being totally Amish or something. "I guess that could work."

We drove along in silence after that, as the road got progressively rougher and I hung on to the door handle, trying not to wince every time we hit a particularly nasty rut. It didn't help that I could feel my soggy jeans getting smashed against my rear end with every bump.

But, as he'd told me, although it seemed as though we'd been driving for much longer, it only took a few more minutes before he pulled off onto a lane marked "Private Property." I hadn't noticed any houses as we drove, so his comment about being in the middle of nowhere seemed to be only the truth.

The lane curved, and at the end of it stood masses of trees, cottonwoods and oaks and sycamores, and what I thought were poplars. All of them were bright with fresh spring-green leaves, sheltering a low, sprawling house built in what I thought was the typical Southwest pueblo style, with rounded edges and thick beams protruding from the sides of the structure. A little ways off was what looked like a detached garage with three bays.

Something about the place seemed to exude a sensation of peace, of harmony with nature and its surroundings. Despite my sodden clothes, my spirits lifted.

"I can get you some sweats to put on while we throw your clothes in the dryer," he said as he got out of the SUV. "Maybe get you a cup of tea, too. You must be cold."

Actually, I was. By that point, the sun had descended almost to the horizon. It would be full dark by the time I got back to my car.

That thought didn't seem very confidence-inspiring, even though Calvin had told me it would be perfectly safe where it was.

"That sounds great," I said, following him along a flagstone path that led through a nicely landscaped yard all done in native, drought-tolerant plants, with large sandstone boulders placed here and there to artistic effect. I wondered if he'd planted the yard or had someone design the layout for him. It seemed very professional.

The interior of the house was cool and smelled faintly of wood smoke. Not a lot of furniture, but all the pieces seemed to have been chosen to exactly fit the Southwest architecture—heavy oak and what I thought might be juniper, spare and simple, like a sun-bleached skull you might find in the desert.

"Hang on a sec," Calvin told me. "I'll go grab some sweats for you."

"I promise I won't sit down on anything," I said, and he flashed me what looked like a genuine grin.

"Thanks."

As I waited in the living room—he'd flicked on the lights, since it was already fairly dim inside —he headed down the hall, presumably to the bedroom. Part of me was dying to see what his room looked like, even as I told myself to stay where I was.

Besides, if I got really lucky, maybe someday I'd get to see that room for myself.

A minute later, he returned, carrying a pair of

dark sweatpants and an oversized Arizona State University sweatshirt. "These will be huge on you," he said, "but at least it's something."

"Thanks," I replied as I took the sweats from him. "I'll just roll up the sleeves."

"The bathroom is down there," he said, pointing.

Right. I nodded and headed in the direction he'd indicated, then went in the bathroom and closed the door. It was only a powder room, with a toilet and a pretty antique wooden cabinet acting as the vanity, complete with a hand-painted sink of Mexican ceramic.

Being a tribal police chief must pay better than I thought.

Or maybe he'd built the place himself, or inherited it. I didn't know, and I certainly wasn't going to ask. Still, I thought it must be a positive sign from the universe that I felt so comfortable in Calvin's house…or at least, I would once I was out of those wet clothes.

I peeled myself out of my wet jeans and T-shirt, then debated for a moment whether I should leave on my bra and panties or go commando. Something about that felt just a little too risky, so I decided to keep them on, although I blotted the bra with one of the hand towels. Honestly, my panties weren't completely soaked, just sort of damp, and so I hoped they'd dry quickly once I was wearing Calvin's sweats.

To my infinite relief, my phone seemed to have survived. The key fob I'd just have to test once I got back to the car, but since the phone appeared intact, I had to hope the fob was similarly none the worse for wear.

After I'd changed—and rolled up the bottoms of the sweatpants and the sleeves of the sweatshirt so I wasn't tripping over myself, then stuck my phone and key fob in the sweatshirt's kangaroo pocket—I wadded my clothes into a ball and went back outside. He was still waiting in the living room, although he reached for the bundle of clothing I carried as soon as I got close.

"Let me throw those in the dryer," he said. "You might as well follow me—the laundry room is off the kitchen, and I'll get the tea going once these have started drying."

That sounded like a sensible plan, so I padded along after him in my bare feet as he headed down the hall toward the kitchen. Like the rest of the house, it seemed pretty luxe for a rural police chief living on his own—polished concrete counters and stainless appliances, including a high-end six-burner Viking monstrosity that I coveted immediately. The kitchen in my own apartment had been updated beautifully, but there just wasn't room for anything quite that lavish.

Calvin disappeared through a door that opened off the kitchen. After a few beeps I assumed came from him pushing his selections on the dryer, he came back in and headed over to the stove so he could collect the kettle that waited there. He filled it and set it down on one of the front burners, then turned back toward me.

"Any particular tea preferences? I think I have some English Breakfast, or there's chamomile, peppermint, Lemon Zinger—"

"Lemon Zinger," I said, figuring that would pep me up a bit. It had always been one of my favorite herbal teas, although my supply was getting low and I'd probably have to mail-order it, since I couldn't find it at the local Walmart.

He got out a couple of mugs and some tea bags. Once that was done, he leaned against the counter and sent me a very direct look.

I did what I could to match his stare. The one good thing about my dunking in the San Ramon River was that it hadn't been deep enough for me to get entirely underwater, so I had to hope my makeup was intact. The ends of my hair had gotten wet, but it was so stick straight that it had just dried back to more or less its natural state.

"Did you sense anything out there?" he asked abruptly.

"Yes," I said, again because I'd resolved to tell

him the truth. Lying would only make me look guilty.

"What did you feel?"

"Fear...pain," I replied. "It wasn't pleasant."

His fingers tapped against the edge of the concrete counter. "No, I guess not. You think it was him?"

Calvin hadn't said who he meant by "him," but I didn't have to ask. "I don't see who else it could be," I replied. "Well, unless you get a lot of people murdered down by the river."

"Not generally, no," he said. "That is, we had a case of drowning one year when a tourist decided it would be a really good idea to go wading in the river after he had a twelve-pack of Coors, but as a general rule, it's a pretty quiet spot."

I reflected that it was quite an accomplishment to drown yourself in a river that wasn't even two feet deep. But maybe there were sections where it wasn't quite as shallow.

"Did you see anything else?"

For a moment, I hesitated. Yes, I'd sworn to tell Calvin the truth, but I didn't know whether I wanted to let him know about that metallic glint I'd detected down amongst the river stones. It could have been nothing—a smashed beer can or something similar. The glinting object had looked smaller than that, though, like a coin or maybe a piece of jewelry.

But then I reminded myself that he was the professional, that just because I'd decided to play Nancy Drew didn't mean I had the right to withhold information about something that might be an important piece of evidence.

"Not in a vision or anything," I said. "But I was just about to pick up something I saw down in the riverbed when you interrupted me."

His brows drew together in a frown I was beginning to recognize. "Why didn't you say something when we were back there?"

"Oh, I don't know…because I'd just fallen in a river? I sort of had other things occupying my mind."

For a second, it looked as though he was going to utter some kind of retort. Then he appeared to think better of it, because he said, "What was it?"

"I don't know for sure. Something metallic, maybe about this big." I held up my hand and made a circle with my thumb and forefinger around the size of a silver dollar. "It's hard to say for sure, because water distorts things."

The kettle began to whistle then, so he went to the stove and turned off the gas. Silence for a moment as he poured hot water into the mugs he'd set out earlier, and then he said, "I'll go back and look in the morning. It's going to be too dark by the time I get you back to your car. I don't know how my deputies and I missed something like that, though."

"Maybe it was closer to one of the rocks, and then the current in the water shifted it as the day went on," I suggested.

"Possibly." He lifted one of the mugs and handed it to me. I took it from him, glad of the warmth of the heavily glazed stoneware beneath my fingers. The sweats he'd loaned me were warm enough, but the tile floor under my bare feet was cooler than I'd expected it to be. "Anyway," he went on, "I'll take a look. And from now on, try to avoid playing amateur detective."

"Because the professional ones are doing such a great job?" I responded, and he shot me a pained glance.

"This isn't TV," he told me. "Things don't get wrapped up neatly in forty-five minutes."

"I don't even watch TV," I said, which might have been a slight exaggeration but close enough to the truth.

Apparently, he chose to ignore that comment, because he said, "I know you think you're trying to help, but you need to let me do my job."

"Fine." I lifted the mug to my lips and took a teeny sip, just because I knew it was still probably too hot to drink anything more than that. "Were you able to find Athene Kappas?"

His lips thinned. Obviously, asking about the

other chief suspect in a murder investigation wasn't what Calvin Standingbear considered leaving him alone to do his job. And even though I could tell I'd annoyed him again, I had to admit that there was something highly satisfying about standing a few feet away and simply looking at him, taking in the high, hard cheekbones and the lashes that were even more night-dark than his hair…the mouth that was just as chiseled as his nose and chin.

Had I ever seen a more gorgeous man?

I doubted it. Or rather, I didn't think I'd ever seen anyone quite so godlike outside the pages of a magazine or maybe on a movie screen.

However, there was nothing particularly godlike about the scowl he sent in my direction. "You know I can't talk to you about that."

"I'm not asking you to tell me what she *said*," I replied, then allowed myself a slightly larger sip of tea. "I only asked if you were able to find her."

He paused, then appeared to decide that minor point wasn't worth quibbling over. "Yes, I found her. As you told me, she's staying at an Airbnb here in town. And I let her know that she needed to stick around, same as I told you."

Only I wasn't guilty. Athene didn't seem to me like the sort of person to fly into a jealous rage and stab someone multiple times, but that didn't mean much. My work with clients—and my own experiences working through my shadow self, or the darker side of my soul that needed to be understood and embraced as yet another part of myself—told me that everyone had sides to their natures they preferred to keep secret.

I had to wonder what Calvin Standingbear's shadows might be.

"I doubt she was too happy about that."

Not even a twitch of his mouth. "I'll take the Fifth on that one."

So, Athene was annoyed that she'd been instructed to cool her heels in tiny Globe for the time being. Well, I couldn't blame her too much. I'd had the store opening preparations to keep me busy, but otherwise, there wasn't much to do. A few restaurants, a few shops, some truly spectacular hiking if you were into that sort of thing. The town did boast a very small, very cute movie theater right downtown, but with only four screens to choose from, you'd run out of viewing options pretty fast if you had to spend any amount of time there.

So much I wanted to ask—whether she'd seemed shocked or sad when she found out about Lucien, what she'd looked like when she got the news, whether she had any suggestions for possible suspects.

Or maybe I didn't want to know that last bit. Athene had never been a fan of mine, and I thought it distinctly possible that she'd throw me under the bus if it meant removing suspicion from herself. Not exactly the most charitable position to take, but over the years, I'd learned that people who considered themselves enlightened—or at least spiritual—could be just as petty as anyone else.

Anyway, it didn't matter what I wanted to know. Calvin clearly planned to remain tight-lipped, and any attempt on my part to pry important information out of him would meet with failure.

So, I decided to try another tack. "Can I come with you tomorrow when you go back to the river to look for that object I found?"

"Now, why would I let you do that?"

"Because you wouldn't even know it was there if I hadn't told you about it," I said reasonably. His tone irritated me, but I wouldn't let him see that he'd gotten under my skin.

He sipped from his oversized mug of tea, dark eyes watching me over the brim. I stared back at him, trying to look as guileless as possible. Actually, I *was* guileless—I didn't know what the object was and whether it would turn out to be important to the case or not, but I figured I had just as much right to be there as anyone else.

"All right," he replied after a long pause. "But

I plan to be out there early. You'll need to meet me at the river at eight o'clock."

Inwardly, I winced. I had never been what you could call a morning person; even a ten o'clock opening time for the store was a bit early for me. However, I vowed to myself that I'd be there to meet Calvin at the river, even if he'd said he was heading out there at dawn.

"I'll bring coffee," I said coolly.

An eyebrow lifted, but he only said, "I take it black."

"Good to know."

We drank our tea in silence after that, and about five minutes later, the dryer beeped, signaling that my clothes were dry. He handed them over to me, and I returned to the powder room so I could change out of my borrowed sweats and into my freshly dried T-shirt, jeans, and socks. My boots were still pretty waterlogged, but I pulled them on anyway, knowing I couldn't possibly walk across the gravel-paved front path barefoot.

And after that, we headed back out to his Durango, and he drove me to the recreation area parking lot where I'd left my car. A "see you at eight," and then he was gone.

A romantic first date, it was not. Or any kind of date. But Calvin had taken me to his house, and I figured that had to signal some kind of progression in our relationship, even if he wouldn't admit to it.

Whistling, I backed out of my parking space. Now all I had to do was help him solve this murder, and we'd be on to something.

9

Medallions and Musings

DRAGGING MYSELF OUT OF BED AT JUST A little past six-thirty took a supreme effort of will, but I told myself that all progress required sacrifice and I needed to suck it up. Archie was not thrilled with me for blasting my hair dryer at the ungodly hour of seven o'clock on a Sunday morning, and watched with a jaundiced eye as I applied eye liner with far more care than I usually did.

"Hot date?" he asked sourly.

I wondered where he'd heard that term. Most of the time, his language was almost too formal, making him sound like a fussy history professor I'd had at Cal State Northridge who always wore tweed jackets, even if it was ninety degrees outside. I'd dropped out after my second year, realizing that college wasn't my true path, but some things had stuck with me.

"No," I said, in tones I intended to be quelling but which merely sounded petulant. "I'm helping Calvin Standingbear with something. That's all."

Archie didn't appear dissuaded by my remark. He sat up on his haunches and glared at me with baleful golden eyes before saying, "The same Calvin Standingbear who took you to his house last night?"

Because when I'd gotten home at a little past seven the evening before, Archie had been waiting right in the entry, tail waving in annoyance at my tardiness. I'd been feeding him his dinner every night at precisely six-fifteen, and he'd been more than a little ticked off that I'd made him wait almost forty-five minutes for his bowl of Special Kitty kibble.

"He took me to his house because it was his fault I fell in the river and got soaked," I replied crisply. "I already told you that. The rest of it is none of your business."

Archie's tail flicked back and forth in annoyance, and he let out a small hiss, but I noticed that he didn't reply, only stalked off toward the living room, which offered the best chance of a pool of sunlight to lie in at that time of day.

Typical.

But at least I didn't have to waste any more time arguing with him. I dabbed on some mascara, finished with lipstick, and gave my reflection a careful inspection. It was entirely possible that I was aiming a little above my pay grade by thinking Calvin would be interested in any kind of a relationship with me, but I told myself that faint heart never won hot police chief.

If nothing else, thinking about how I could flirt with him while not really flirting with him was a good way to distract myself from Lucien's murder.

At that hour, Cloud Coffee was packed. Luckily, I'd given myself some extra time, so even though it took nearly fifteen minutes for me to get two coffees and an impulse buy of a cheese danish for Calvin and a croissant for myself, it was still just twenty minutes to eight by the time I headed east on Highway 70 for my rendezvous.

Instead of parking in the lot, I followed the forest road to the spot where he'd left his San Ramon tribal P.D. SUV the day before. My Volkswagen Beetle didn't seem too happy about being driven over such rough terrain, but I pulled into the wide spot in the road I remembered without suffering too much damage. A minute later, Calvin appeared and parked next to me.

I grabbed the carry-out tray with the two coffees and the bag of breakfast pastries, hoping as I did so that I hadn't screwed up by getting him a cheese danish. For all I knew, he was gluten-free and lactose-intolerant.

No, wait—he'd refused my offer of a glass of wine at the store opening, but I knew I'd seen him eat some cheese and crackers, so I guessed I was safe on that front.

"Breakfast!" I said, brandishing the bag.

He removed the aviator-style sunglasses he was wearing and looked at the white paper sack. "I didn't ask for breakfast."

"No," I said cheerfully, "but I was hungry, and I figured I might as well get you something. If you don't want it, I'll take it back home with me."

"What is it?"

"Cheese danish."

His expression brightened noticeably. "My favorite. From Cloud Coffee?"

"Of course."

He took the bag from me and extracted the danish, then accepted the venti black coffee I'd gotten for him as I reflected that sometimes it was a good thing to have intuition about people. It looked as though the breakfast offering might have softened him up a bit.

For a few minutes, we ate and drank in silence, both of us obviously acknowledging that it was better to get fortified before we headed down to the river. Then he swallowed the rest of his coffee and brushed his free hand on the leg of his khaki uniform pants.

"Almost ready?"

I nodded. "Just a bit more cappuccino for me."

I drank down the last inch or so of my coffee before stuffing the empty cup in the bag that had held the pastries. Then I held it open so Calvin could dispose of his trash the same way. That matter handled, I headed over to my Beetle and stowed the bag on the floor in front of the passenger seat.

"Okay, now I'm ready."

He didn't reply, only tilted his head as if to indicate I should follow him through the cottonwood grove and on to the little beach that apparently was the last thing Lucien Dumond had seen before he departed this mortal coil. Dead leaves left over from the previous autumn crunched beneath our feet as we made our way between the trees. It looked very different that morning with the bright sunlight slanting through the greenery overhead, and I found my mood much lighter than it had been, even if our reason for being there was pretty grim.

We emerged onto the beach, and I took the lead. "Over here," I said, pausing at the water's edge and doing my best to point toward the spot where I'd seen the metal object. My boots still hadn't dried out completely from their dunking the day before, and I really wasn't looking forward to getting them soaked all over again.

Calvin, however, didn't seem to care. Or rather, he'd come prepared; he stopped and rolled up his khaki trousers, revealing a pair of rubber work boots underneath. After shoving his pants into the tops of the boots, he strode out to the spot I'd indicated and looked down into the water.

"I see it," he said. Another slight delay as he also rolled up his sleeves—I guessed that the big, sporty watch he wore had to be waterproof, or at least water-resistant—slipped on a latex glove, and then reached down into the water.

I watched, holding my breath, as he scrabbled around in the mud and rocks at the bottom of the river. It was just deep enough that, even with his sleeves rolled up, he still splashed the edges of the fabric.

But then he pulled his arm out of the water and held it out, hand open. Lying against his glove-covered palm was a round silver medallion, one that was engraved with a stylized half moon on one half and a tree with spreading branches on the other.

My breath sucked in, and Calvin gave me a questioning glance.

"You recognize this?"

I nodded. "It's the symbol of GLANG."

"What's GLANG?"

"Athene didn't tell you?"

"It didn't come up."

All right, then. Still, I wasn't a member, and whatever suspicious activity the necromancers' guild might have been involved in, it wasn't my problem. "It stands for 'Greater Los Angeles Necromancers' Guild.'"

"Necro—" Calvin broke off there, expression dubious. "You're joking, right?"

"Oh, it's no joke," I said. "They're part of the reason why I ended up in Globe. I mean, Lucien was most of the reason, but he wouldn't have been nearly as scary if he didn't have thirty other sorcerers as backup."

Looking grim, Calvin splashed his way back to shore. Since I hadn't actually ventured out into the water, all I had to do was take a couple of steps to be standing on dry land. He waited for me there, the silver medallion gleaming in his hand. "He threatened you?"

"He made it pretty obvious that he didn't like any competition. Not that I do the sort of magic that GLANG dabbles in," I added hastily. The last thing I wanted was for Calvin to think I'd been brewing eye of newt and toe of frog or something. "But he didn't like that I was taking clients away from him. Or at least, he thought I was poaching clients. I really wasn't, but Lucien was never the type of person to allow reality to interfere with his view of the universe."

"And yet he came all the way here to ask you to come back."

"Because he did the math in his head and decided it would be better for him—and GLANG —if I was working for them. Too bad I've never been much of a joiner."

Calvin absorbed this bit of information in silence. I'd noticed that about him; he wasn't afraid to be quiet and think something through before he commented on it. I had to say, it was a nice change of pace from a lot of the guys in L.A. I'd known, the ones who barely came up for air because they were so busy talking your head off about how wonderful they were.

Hefting the medallion in his palm, he asked, "Did everyone in GLANG have one of these?"

Good question. I racked my brain, trying to recall any of my interactions with the members of the guild. Lucien liked to wear bracelets and earrings and rings, but the only pendant I'd ever seen hanging from his neck had been a heavy silver version of the Scorpio symbol. He was so proud of being a double Scorpio.

And the couple of times I'd been to his house in Encino, I'd seen a few more of the GLANG-sters, as I sometimes thought of Lucien's followers, but I couldn't recall if any of them had been wearing a pendant similar to the one Calvin held now. They'd all had on black clothing, loose pants and band-collared shirts for the men, loose but low-cut tank-style dresses for the women. If they'd been wearing any kind of jewelry around their necks, you'd think I would have noticed.

Come to think of it….

"The only person I ever saw wearing one was Athene Kappas," I said, and Calvin gave a nod. Not a satisfied one, exactly, but as if that piece of information corroborated what he'd already suspected. Silently, he took a small baggie out of his pants pocket—did he have an inexhaustible supply of them in there?—and then dropped the medallion inside. That task handled, he put the baggie with its piece of evidence in his pocket before removing the latex glove he wore.

"I'll take this back to the station and check it for fingerprints. Probably a long shot because of it being in the water overnight, but you never know."

"And then…?" I prompted.

Dark eyes met mine. "You know what I've told you about ongoing police investigations."

Of course. Still, I wouldn't be dissuaded that easily. "Okay, you don't have to tell me outright. Just blink once if I'm right."

"Selena, this isn't junior high."

I refused to be offended. "I know. But you wouldn't have this piece of evidence at all if it weren't for my help, so can't you give me just a little bit?"

An unwilling chuckle escaped his lips. "You're very persistent, aren't you?"

"I don't know about that," I said. "It's just...I want to know what happened. No, I *need* to know what happened, because otherwise, everyone's going to keep on thinking that I had something to do with Lucien's murder even if you don't have enough evidence to charge me. And that's no way to start a new life in a new town."

"Well, that's true." Calvin's expression was almost sympathetic. He hesitated a moment before saying, "After I check the medallion for fingerprints, I'm going to talk to Athene Kappas again. Whether or not she'll give me any actionable information is, of course, up to her. Is that enough for you?"

I supposed it would have to be. As easygoing as Calvin was being right now, I doubted he'd let me do a ride-along on that particular interview. "It is for now," I replied, and he chuckled again.

"All right, you do have a vested interest in all this. I get it."

"And you don't think I'm guilty?"

His gaze caught mine and held. A little shiver went through me, the kind of pleasant thrill I might get from touching a nicely charged crystal.

Actually, it was way more than that. I just

didn't know whether he felt any of the same things I did.

"No," he said quietly. "I don't think you are."

It turned out that I really didn't need Calvin to give me the skinny on what was going on, not when I had Josie Woodrow on my side.

She rang the buzzer for the back entrance off the shop, since it was Sunday and the store was closed. I hurried down the stairs, wondering who could be calling and inwardly hoping it was Calvin Standingbear.

No such luck…but a little gossip with Josie wasn't a bad second place.

I asked her if she wanted some iced tea, and of course, she accepted. Glass in hand, she settled on my couch, eyes alight with anticipation.

"I talked to Betsy, my friend with the Airbnb," she told me in confidential tones. "It seems the woman staying there left this morning."

"'Left'?" I repeated. "But I thought Calvin Standingbear told her she had to stay in town."

Josie didn't exactly say, "aha!", but an air of triumph about her after hearing that news told me I'd just dropped a piece of important information. Damn it. One problem with being a Gemini— you tended to run at the mouth.

"Well, she's gone," Josie said. "Betsy said the place was a mess, too—towels on the floor in the bathroom, half the bedclothes on the floor as well, sink full of dishes. And she said it stank so much of incense, she wasn't sure whether she was ever going to get the smell out of the upholstery."

I hoped Betsy had gotten a hefty deposit from Lucien and Athene. Somehow, I guessed she probably wouldn't have any other way of covering her cleaning costs. Which led me to wonder who—if anyone—he'd designated as the heir to his not-inconsiderable fortune. He didn't have any children, but his parents were still alive. And I knew he had a younger brother named Eugene, who'd followed in their father's footsteps and was a dentist of some sort, although I didn't know much more than that. I'd gotten the impression he wasn't much involved in Lucien's life, which I supposed was understandable.

"Oh, that's terrible," I said. "I suppose if Athene left in a hurry, that would explain the mess, but still."

Josie sipped some of her iced tea. "It may explain it, but it certainly doesn't excuse it. Betsy has her cleaning gal over there now, so I hope she can get the place straightened up without too much trouble. But where do you think she could have gone?" she went on, barely stopping to take a breath before changing the subject.

I had to guess that the "she" in Josie's question wasn't a reference to Betsy's cleaning lady. "I have no idea. I mean, she didn't have access to Lucien's car, but I suppose she could have called Travis Cox to give her a ride somewhere."

That suggestion made her eyes light up. "You know, that's exactly it. We should call Calvin to let him know he should question Travis!"

"I'm pretty sure Calvin can figure that out for himself," I responded. While he'd been friendly enough during our meeting earlier that morning, he'd also given me the impression that he wouldn't appreciate too much more interference on my part. "In fact, since he said he was going to talk to her again this morning, it's probably a pretty safe bet that he's already discovered she's missing and has put two and two together."

"Was there a particular reason why he wanted to talk to her again so soon?"

There, I hesitated. I could have tried to tell myself I was only having a cozy gossip with a friend, but at the bottom of it all, this was still a very fresh murder investigation. The irritation Calvin had showed earlier over my attempts to get more information told me all I needed to know about how he'd feel if I started spreading every detail of the inquiry all over town.

"Oh, I think he probably just wanted to go over a few things. She's his only lead, after all."

This reply seemed to satisfy Josie, because she nodded and drank some more iced tea. Then she said, "Well, this Athene person is going to stick out like a sore thumb here in Globe. I'm sure someone will spot her soon enough."

Normally, I would have agreed with Josie's rosy outlook on the situation. I knew how cagey Athene could be, however, and so I had no way of knowing if she'd simply decided to relocate to another Airbnb or hotel in town, or whether she really had gotten Travis to drive her to the airport.

No, strike that. I had lots of ways of finding out things—none of which I could employ while Josie Woodrow was hanging out in my apartment.

"Probably," I said. "Luckily, she's Calvin's problem, not mine."

Those words made Josie tilt her head and give me a curious look. "Are you sure of that? Because if she's really a murderer...and the jealous type...."

I knew I had to cut off that line of thinking before she allowed it to go any further. "Athene Kappas is not the jealous type," I said. "I *maybe* could see her killing Lucien over a business disagreement or something like that, but she wouldn't have cared if there was anything going on between him and another woman. In fact, there were things going on between him and plenty of other women, come to think of it."

"Playboy type," Josie remarked, disapproval clear in her voice. "I can't see why. Betsy said he wasn't an attractive man at *all*."

No, feature for feature, he wasn't. Since I'd been immune to his particular brand of charm, I could see why Josie's friend would have made such an observation about him. I shrugged and drank some of my iced tea. "For some people, it's about power and money, not looks."

The "hmph" sound Josie made told me all I needed to know about her opinion on the subject. I had to agree with her. Or rather, a man's personality and looks in combination were what I found attractive, not how much money he had or his influence over other people.

And although I'd done my best not to think about him, I couldn't quite keep my thoughts from straying to Calvin Standingbear, to the beautifully secluded property he called home. Not so long ago, I probably wouldn't have been able to see the charm in a place so perfectly suited to both its landscape and the man who lived there, but once I'd seen Calvin at home, I honestly couldn't imagine him anywhere else. He seemed one with the place, comfortable with where he was in the world.

Was there anything more attractive than that?

"Anyway," I went on, pushing aside the image of him leaning up against the counter in his kitchen, the flash of the moon-phase tattoo on his forearm as he lifted his mug of Lemon Zinger to take a sip, "none of us knows for sure if Athene is the only suspect. Besides me," I added, as Josie's eyebrow took on a tilt and she looked as though she was about to protest.

"Oh, you're not *really* a suspect," she said, voice firm with conviction. "Anyone can see you're not capable of such a thing. I'm sure Calvin only considered you at all because you're the only person here in town who knew the victim."

Since he'd said basically the same thing to me already, I just nodded. "I hope he can find Athene. I'm not sure what she was thinking—taking off like this only makes her look more guilty."

To my surprise, Josie looked almost sympathetic. "She was probably feeling desperate. Alone in a strange town, the man who was her business partner murdered...I have a feeling she couldn't have been thinking straight."

If it had been anyone else, I might have agreed. However, Athene Kappas seemed like one of the last people who would lose her cool like that. Nothing ever seemed to ruffle her.

"I hope that's all it is," I said, and decided to leave it there. After all, we could spend the entire afternoon speculating and wouldn't be any closer to the truth.

Josie seemed to realize I didn't have much

more to say on the topic, because she excused herself a few minutes later, saying she had a pre-listing inspection she needed to do. I walked her to the front of the apartment and said goodbye, then closed the door behind her while I released a silent sigh of relief.

Now I could get to work.

10

On the Ball

ARCHIE WAS ASLEEP IN HIS BED WHEN I entered the office. He cracked an eyelid as I made my way over to the table that held my altar, but didn't seem otherwise inclined to pay much attention to what I was doing.

Good. I could work with an audience, but I preferred not to.

Because the pendulum had worked so well for me when I was looking for evidence along the San Ramon River, I figured I'd go ahead and start there. If that didn't work, there were my Tarot cards, or my rune stones. If neither of those provided any illumination, then I'd have to bring in the big guns, but I had to hope I wouldn't be pushed to that resort.

I went to the closet and got out the pendulum cloth I used for this sort of work, then lifted a clear quartz pendulum from inside the carved box where I normally kept it. For a moment, I stood there quietly, letting it dangle from my hand as I adjusted my energies from the level required for gossiping with a friend to what I needed in order to pursue a slightly more esoteric goal.

Next, to fix my intentions. I wasn't trying to hunt down Athene Kappas to bring her to justice. That was Calvin's job, not mine...if she was even guilty in the first place. No, what I really wanted to know was whether any harm had come to her, or whether she was even still in Globe at all.

Show me Athene, I thought. Not literally, of course; a pendulum wouldn't grant me any visions. But it could spell out clues that would guide me to her.

For a second or two, the pendulum hung straight down, without even a hint of any movement. Then it began to swing in a circle, slowly at first, then faster and faster until it became almost a blur.

I'd never seen it do that before. In fact, I had to reach out and grab the thing before it tore itself from my hand and went flying across the room.

What in the world...?

All right, maybe the pendulum hadn't been the best choice for this particular quest.

I secured it in its box, then reached for another box, the one that held my two favorite decks of Tarot cards. For this particular question, which required a bit of far-seeing, I thought the crow deck was probably my best choice.

Holding the words, *Show me Athene,* once again in my mind, I pulled a card from the deck.

The Queen of Swords, reversed.

Well, maybe I was being a bit too literal. Or rather, the cards were, since the Queen of Swords in the upside-down position could refer to a woman who seemed cold-hearted and—dare I say it?—bitchy, both words I'd used to mentally describe the woman in question.

I shuffled the deck again, asking it to show me where Athene had gone. The next two cards were the two of cups and the four of wands, neither of which seemed applicable to the current situation.

Maybe I should try my moon deck.

However, when it turned up the Queen of Swords once again, I guessed that the Tarot just wasn't operating on the correct wavelength for me.

I slid both decks into their protective bags and returned them to their box. Next to it stood my crystal ball, resting on the pretty stand of four crescent moons that I'd bought on Etsy a while back.

Looked like it was time to bring in the big guns, since I had a feeling my rune stones wouldn't be any more helpful than the pendulum and the Tarot cards had proved to be.

Reluctantly, I reached for the ball and pulled it closer to where I stood. Its surface was cool against my fingertips, and I made myself take a breath.

I wasn't a medium, wasn't someone who communed with the dead. What I was about to do was subtly different...but that difference mattered.

Calling on one's ancestors for guidance has always been a big part of witchcraft going back centuries, if even longer than that. I never knew my maternal grandmother, because she died of breast cancer when my mother was only twenty, three years before she even had me. But when I first picked up my crystal ball and laid my hands on it, asking for guidance from the spirit world, it had been Ellen Marx staring back at me from within the crystal.

Actually, at first I hadn't even realized it was her, because the face of the woman who'd reached out to make that connection looked just as young as mine, and most of the pictures I'd seen of her had been when she was in her thirties and forties, raising her young daughter alone after her husband—my grandfather—walked out. It had always seemed grossly unfair to me that she'd gone through so much, only to lose her life to cancer before she was even fifty years old, but she didn't seem too bitter about it.

Most of the time, I tried my best to get the answers I needed through other means of divination. I hadn't seen the need to reach out to Grandma Ellen when making the decision to move to Globe, since the pendulum and the Tarot cards had made it pretty damn clear where I was supposed to go.

This time, though, I thought I needed some extra help. I didn't know what force was clouding Athene's location, but I didn't seem able to break through that veil on my own.

The blue eyes looking out at me from within the crystal ball were almost identical to my own. All three generations of Marx women had those same eyes, although my hair was much darker, thanks to the genes I'd inherited from my father, a guitarist in a failed hair band that my mother had hooked up with back in the early '90s.

"You moved," my grandmother said, her tone almost but not quite accusing.

"I thought it was time for a change of pace."

Her tawny brows lifted, although she refrained from commenting. I never could tell exactly how much she knew of what was going on in my life—or in my head—although it seemed obvious to me that she caught enough to know about any major life changes. "What do you need, Selena?"

As usual, there was something almost impatient about her manner, as if she had a packed schedule in the afterlife and kept getting dragged away from it by my constant interruptions. Maybe she did. She never told me much about what she did with her time when she wasn't hanging out in the crystal ball and dispensing bits of advice, so far all I knew, she spent her days lying poolside while heavenly cabana boys brought her mai tais or something.

"I'm trying to find someone," I said. "Her name is Athene Kappas. She was Lucien Dumond's business partner."

A flicker of distaste flared in my grandmother's eyes. "Oh, he's a nasty piece of work. Odd that he didn't get immediately recycled."

Her term for people being sent back to Earth to live another life. I didn't know why my grandmother had been allowed to stay in the afterlife—or the summerlands, if you wanted to use the ancient phrase—rather than being sent back to live all over again. I supposed it was possible that she'd reached the end of her karmic journey, and was now allowed to stay in her version of heaven and dispense advice.

"Is he up there?" I asked next. I tended to think of the summerlands as "up," although directions as mortals thought of them really weren't a thing when it came to describing the etheric planes. And it seemed strange to me that Lucien would be hanging around there when I doubted he was anywhere close to the end of his travels on the wheel of existence.

A pause, and then Grandma Ellen said, "No. At least, I didn't sense him come through. I suppose I could have missed it. I see a lot, but I don't see everything."

"Well, here's hoping he evolves a bit on the next go-'round, whenever that is," I said lightly. "Anyway, Athene and I are the main suspects in his murder, and now that she's missing—"

"Why would anyone suspect you of murdering Lucien Dumond?" Grandma Ellen broke in. "You're the kind of person who puts spiders out rather than kill them."

True enough. I wouldn't say there weren't a few times when I'd been sorely tempted to squish a particularly scary specimen, but I'd told myself to be brave and let the spider carry on…just not in my bedroom or my shower. Yet another downside to being in a place where no one knew me very well. Back in L.A., I probably would have had plenty of people who could vouch for my pacifist nature.

"Lucien and I had an argument that was overheard," I said briefly. "It's all right, though—the police chief doesn't think I did it. But we need to talk to Athene and find out what she's hiding."

"Hmm," my grandmother said, and frowned. Her eyes closed, showing off her thick eyelashes—

lashes I'd also inherited. It was always odd to look at her youthful face and see much of myself in her —the oval face and full mouth, the just slightly longish nose—but at the same time, it was easier to recognize those attributes because I was looking at a face that didn't seem any older than mine.

Her silence stretched on for a minute, and then another. I held myself still, knowing I didn't dare interrupt as she was trying to focus, even while I wished I could see something of what she was seeing as she sat there on the etheric plane and reached out with senses no earthly being possessed.

"Athene is still nearby," she said at length. "I can feel her vibrations not too far from you."

A relieved breath slipped past my lips. That was something. At least it seemed as if my visions of her escaping town in an Uber and flying back to Los Angeles had been nothing more than worst-case fears.

"Where is she?"

"I can't say exactly." Once again, her brows knotted together. "I know it's someplace close, and yet I can't see anything clearly. It's as if a mist surrounds her, hiding her from my sight."

That sounded to me as if Athene had cast some sort of spell to hide herself from any pursuers. I suppose that made sense, especially if she hadn't yet been able to come up with a means of getting herself physically away from Globe.

But why would she do such a thing in the first place? Didn't she know how guilty that made her look?

Maybe it's because she is guilty, I thought. *She could have gone to ground to get herself some breathing room. Maybe she realized this morning that her medallion was missing, and it was only a matter of time before Calvin or his deputies found it and realized it was a piece of evidence that couldn't be ignored.*

That all sounded sensible enough, and yet I still couldn't shake the feeling I'd missed something vitally important.

"How close is she?" I asked next, knowing I sounded a bit too desperate. "Like, right down the street? The other side of town? Out at the casino/hotel?"

My grandmother only smiled. "I'm not a GPS device, Selena. I can tell she's around somewhere not too far away, but that's the only thing I can sense. You'll have to do the rest of the work yourself."

Because I already had plenty of experience with the limitations of otherworldly help, I wasn't too upset by her comment. And the situation could have been much worse. I could have been trying to track down Athene in my old neighborhood back in West L.A., an area full of apartment buildings and duplexes and hotels, rather than quiet little Globe.

"Well, thanks, Grandma," I said. "I'll see what I can find out."

Her head tilted slightly. "How's the love life?"

"The same," I replied. Which I supposed was mostly the truth. I'd met someone I found interesting, but I couldn't tell whether he thought I was equally interesting. We'd certainly not gone on anything remotely resembling a date, unless you counted getting dunked in the river.

Anyway, I didn't plan to tell my grandmother any of that, partly because there wasn't much to tell, and partly because I didn't want to send the conversation along a route where she'd be likely to ask me a lot of questions. Also, it was entirely possible she knew all about Calvin if she'd been taking a peek at my life to see what I was up to. No point in wasting any more time.

A little twinkle in her blue eyes told me she knew I was lying, or at least omitting parts of the truth. But she only said, "Ah, well, maybe it will pick up now that you're out of Los Angeles. The energy there was never very good for you."

Now you tell me, I thought, but I let it go. Better to focus on the present, rather than a past that couldn't be changed.

"We'll see," I said lightly. "Thanks, Grandma Ellen."

"That's what I'm here for."

She disappeared from the crystal ball, and I reached for the piece of dark green silk I used to cover it when it wasn't in use.

Afterward, I headed back out to the living room and peeked through the blinds on one of the front windows. As usual, there wasn't much to see; downtown Globe wasn't a hotbed of activity on the best of days, and on Sunday afternoon, when almost everything except the movie theater and a couple of restaurants were closed, it might as well have been a ghost town.

Hmm.

Grandma Ellen had said she didn't sense Lucien on her plane, which might or might not have meant much. Evolved spirits such as hers could see a lot, but they weren't omniscient.

Still, I couldn't help being a bit troubled. When a life was violently cut short the way his was, that spirit could remain on the earthly plane, haunting the place wherever they'd met their end.

Was that what I'd felt when I'd walked along the bank of the San Ramon River? Had it been Lucien Dumond's ghost haunting the isolated spot? When I sensed those ripples of fear and pain, I'd thought they were only psychic echoes from the moment when he'd died…but maybe it had been something much worse.

A shiver inched its way down my spine, although I told myself ghosts were nothing to fear. Encountering one could be disconcerting, but a ghost couldn't actually hurt you.

Supposedly.

I put that thought aside for the moment, figuring I could revisit it once I'd gotten the whole Athene problem worked out. If she was still in the area, there weren't many places she could have gone to ground. Globe had exactly three hotels— a Best Western and a Holiday Inn Express near the intersection of Highway 70 and Highway 60, and a shabby little motel called the Dew Drop Inn out on the western edge of town. None of them seemed like the sort of place where she would hole up, but beggars couldn't be choosers. It shouldn't take me too long to call each hotel and—

And nothing. I wasn't a cop or even a private investigator; it wasn't as though I could call any of the hotels in question and ask whether a woman matching Athene Kappas' description had checked in there earlier in the day.

Also, I guessed that Calvin would have checked both those places just as soon as he realized his other suspect had bolted. While I didn't expect him to keep me abreast of every development in the case, I had a feeling he would have told me he'd located Athene.

So…she had to have gone someplace else. Another Airbnb or some kind of vacation rental? That seemed like the likeliest explanation, but again, I figured Calvin must have checked any place like that as well. And it wasn't as if Athene knew anyone in Globe; she couldn't have headed over to a friend's house.

Frowning, I turned away from the window. I didn't want to bother Josie when I knew she had a house pre-inspection to manage—it might have been Sunday, but that didn't matter to Josie Woodrow—but on the other hand, she seemed like the best person to ask whether she knew of anyone who was listing vacation rentals on Craigslist or something, the kind of place Calvin might not think immediately to check.

For some reason, Hazel's face flashed into my mind. No, she hadn't lived in Globe her entire life like Josie, but she'd been there for more than seven years and pretty much knew everyone as well. And if I called her, then I wouldn't have to bug Josie while she was trying to work.

I got my phone from my purse and pushed the "call" button next to Hazel's name on my contacts list. It rang a couple of times, and I wondered if she was going to pick up. After all, the day was a beautiful one, and I thought it was entirely possible she'd decided to go hiking, maybe bring along a palette for some *plein air* painting. She had several pieces in the town's one and only art gallery, and I'd been eyeing her sunset vision of the San Ramon river, all gold-brushed cottonwoods and warm, lovely tones. It would look gorgeous in my living room.

But then her voice came through my iPhone's speaker. "Hi, Selena. What's up?"

She sounded almost tense, which was very unlike Hazel. Small-town life suited her, and she tended to be relaxed and easygoing no matter what the situation. My spider-sense tingled a little, but I only said, "Hi, Hazel. This is going to sound like a weird question, but do you know of anyone in town who's recently started renting out their house as an Airbnb or other kind of vacation rental, someone Calvin might not know about? It's just that my friend Athene has gone missing, and—"

A long pause. Then Hazel said, "She told me you'd probably figure it out."

"'She'?" I repeated, not sure what she'd meant by that remark.

"Athene Kappas," Hazel said. "She's here."

11

Questions and Answers

ATHENE DEFINITELY DIDN'T LOOK LIKE HER normal in-command self. Her long, near-black hair had been pulled back into a barrette rather than flowing down her back the way she usually wore it, and her face was bare of makeup. Shadows darkened the skin under her eyes.

"I put my second bedroom on Craigslist just a day ago," Hazel said as she handed me a glass of iced tea and poured more for Athene. Judging by the way Athene's hand shook as she held out the glass, I had a feeling she really didn't need any more caffeine.

Not that I was going to say anything. If anyone had earned the right to be jittery, it was Athene Kappas.

"Things have been a little tight lately," Hazel went on, "so I figured I might as well give it a try.

I was looking for more of a long-term renter, but—"

"But I told her I'd pay her for a month's worth of renting the room," Athene cut in. "I needed a place to think."

"What happened?" I asked. She didn't look like someone who'd just committed a violent murder, but appearances weren't everything.

But while her aura spiked with the yellow and pale orange of worry, I didn't see any gray and black guilty edges to it. While it wasn't too hard to manage your expressions, it was very difficult to change your aura.

She rubbed her hand over the fabric of the long black skirt she wore. I didn't think I'd ever seen Athene wear anything but black.

"Violet showed up," she said, her full mouth compressing to a flat line.

I racked my brains, trying to remember who Violet was. Lucien had so many groupies hanging around, it was hard to keep track of them all. I had a vague recollection of a slight girl with pale blonde hair, but I couldn't recall for sure if the girl in my memory was Violet or another one of Lucien's hangers-on.

Apparently seeing my mystification, Athene gave me a grim smile. "Violet Clarke. One of Lucien's little fans...and just barely legal. She's obsessed with him. He told her where he was going, the idiot, and she followed us here."

Hazel had been watching our exchange, expression one of worry...and a little confusion. "Where is Violet now?"

"Who knows?" Athene said with a lift of her shoulders. "She and Lucien had their little ritual on Friday night, and then they took off together."

Ritual. I recalled what Josie had said about the loud, tribal music and the scent of incense that had permeated the place. I'd thought Athene and Lucien were practicing sex magic, but it sounded as if it must have been Violet instead.

Who knows what my face did as I reacted to that disturbing mental image, but Athene must have picked up on it, because she gave me a little smirk before drinking some more of her iced tea.

"No, it wasn't me," she said. "Lucien and I were always all business. I went into my bedroom —that was part of the reason why we rented that particular Airbnb...it had two bedrooms...and left them to their business. When they were done, Lucien came and knocked on my door and told me they were headed out. They'd gotten it into their heads that they wanted to perform another ritual out in the woods, next to the river, to pick up some of its energy." Another swallow of tea, and she finished, "That was the last time I ever saw him."

"Why didn't you tell Calvin that?" I asked. True, the girl in question didn't seem like anyone who would be capable of violent murder, but I knew Calvin would still want to talk to her. "You probably wouldn't be a suspect anymore. I mean, if Violet and Lucien were alone together by the river…." The words trailed off, but I knew she must have gotten my meaning.

She shook her head. "I suppose I wanted to protect her. She's so young, and she's gotten herself caught up in something she really doesn't understand."

"But if she's guilty—" Hazel began.

"I can't believe that," Athene said, before adding with a bitter little smile, "Not because I believe in the fundamental goodness of human nature or anything so simple, but because Violet simply isn't strong enough to have overcome a man like Lucien. A girl who's barely five foot three and maybe weighs a hundred pounds wringing wet would be no match for a man in the prime of life."

On the surface, maybe not. But if Violet had been driven into a jealous rage because Lucien had come to Globe to fetch me….

That scenario didn't seem terribly plausible. For one thing, they'd participated in ritual sex that very night, so Violet should have been able to tell Lucien still desired her. Or had she flown into a passion after realizing he'd only used her sexual energy to work his magic, and he didn't care anything about her?

Since I didn't know the girl, I had a hard time answering either of those questions.

"And she wasn't all that strong magically, either," Athene said. "The simplest of Lucien's spells could have snapped her in two, if that had been his intention."

"'Magically'?" Hazel repeated, her expression now torn between amusement and skepticism. "I mean, I know you're a witch, Selena, but—"

"Yes, *magic*," Athene said, her tone now brisk, as if she was glad of the chance to school her temporary landlady. "I'm not saying you need to believe in it, because it's real whether you believe in it or not, but we're all practitioners. Some stronger than others"—she gave me the faintest of nods, as if acknowledging that I wasn't exactly a hack—"but we all have access to it, in one degree or another. Violet has just begun her training, and while she might have some skill in time, she is certainly no match for Lucien."

"Have you seen her?" I asked.

"No. She never came back to the Airbnb. That is, she never came inside the house. Her car was gone, so I assume she must have come back to get it, but I never saw her. When I woke up the next morning, I was a little surprised to see neither of them were there, although I thought they must have stayed out all night." Something that wasn't quite a sigh escaped her pale lips. "It wouldn't have been the first time."

I probably didn't want to know what had kept Lucien out all those other nights. "What kind of car was she driving?"

"A red BMW convertible." Another of those humorless smiles. "Her parents have money."

Of course they did. Lucien just loved to lure rich acolytes to him so he could charge them for classes and seminars and retreats, books and amulets and whatever else he could use to get his hands on their money. I found the whole thing distasteful—practice of the craft should never be tied to how much cash you have on hand—but then again, they were all individuals with free will. They could have seen how morally bankrupt his practices were and moved on to something more personally and karmicly rewarding.

"Well, a red BMW should stand out in Globe," Hazel said.

I couldn't argue with her remark, not when my own much more modest metallic blue Beetle had gotten its share of lifted eyebrows as I drove around town. "That's for sure. I think we'd better let Calvin know to keep an eye out for it—if Violet is even still in the area."

My comment made Athene shoot me a

knowing glance, as if she'd already guessed why I was on a first-name basis with the chief of the San Ramon tribal police department. "Probably should give him a description, too—Violet is nineteen, long blonde hair, blue eyes, short and slender. She was wearing a black dress the last time I saw her, but she might have changed since then."

Nineteen. I wanted to shudder at the thought of a girl so young hooking up with someone who was literally twice her age—actually a bit more, come to think of it. And I also wondered what the hell her parents were thinking, to let her run in that kind of company.

But, as Athene had said, Violet was a legal adult. I had a feeling her parents didn't pay nearly as much attention to her as they probably should, and that was why she'd gotten mixed up with Lucien and GLANG in the first place.

"And let Chief Lewis know, too," Hazel put in. "I know Calvin's working the case because the murder happened on tribal land, but there's probably a greater chance Violet's somewhere in Globe —if she's still around at all."

Right. I was so focused on Calvin Standing-bear, I tended to forget that Globe had its own chief of police, Henry Lewis. Our paths had only crossed once, and he seemed just about the opposite of Calvin, a buzz-cut ex-Marine who clearly had little use for a woman who'd moved into his town and brought her crazy L.A. woo-woo with her.

"I guess so," I said, the lack of enthusiasm in my tone so obvious, Hazel actually chuckled.

"Yeah, I know. And actually, if you tell Calvin, then he'll probably get in contact with Chief Lewis, and then you don't have to worry about talking to him."

That sounded like a much better plan. Even if Violet wasn't a suspect—and I still thought she might be, no matter what Athene had to say on the matter—she was probably the last person who'd seen Lucien Dumond alive, and therefore she'd have information to provide that no one else would.

"Don't tell him you found me," Athene said next, her tone almost pleading.

"He's going to find out sooner or later," I told her. "You're innocent, so you don't have anything to worry about."

The look she gave me after I delivered that remark was almost pitying, as if she couldn't believe anyone could live almost three decades on this planet and still be so naïve. And all right, I had to admit that I generally tried to believe the best about people until they proved me horribly wrong, but still, I could tell Athene hadn't killed Lucien, and so it seemed plausible enough to think that Calvin Standingbear would see that truth as well.

"Besides," I hurried on, "once he hears about Violet, he's going to want to talk to her, and you'll be off the hook for a bit."

"That might be true," Athene said. "But I can't cool my heels here indefinitely. With Lucien gone"—she stopped there and pulled in a breath, a suspicious glint entering her dark eyes—"there's a lot that needs to be done. I was his business partner, so it falls to me to handle the practical side of things. I need to be cleared of suspicion so I can manage the execution of his estate, assure everyone in GLANG that the organization will continue, and take care of any other legal or practical matters that need to be addressed."

Her tone had grown crisper during that speech, as if thinking about all the things that had to be done had helped to smooth some of the rough edges of her grief. Actually, since Athene was such a pragmatic, take-charge sort of person, I had a feeling that's exactly what was going on. I couldn't even blame her; it always helped to have something to distract you from your grief.

"All the more reason to let Calvin know about Violet," I said. "And honestly, he can't be that angry about you relocating from the Airbnb to here. Like you said, you needed some space to think, but it's not as if you left Globe. You were still doing what he told you to do."

An unwilling smile pulled at her mouth. "Have you always been this good at rationalization?"

"Libra ascendant," I told her cheerfully. "I excel at it."

And I pulled out my phone.

When he appeared at Hazel's house, Calvin didn't look too thrilled that I'd managed to locate his runaway murder suspect. His dark eyes met mine and held for a moment, as if telling me that we'd discuss this later.

Which was fine by me, if it meant we'd have a chance to be alone together and talk.

But after that brief, unspoken exchange, he was all business. He declined Hazel's offer of a glass of iced tea and took a seat in the living room's only unoccupied chair, a small hard-backed thing that creaked uncomfortably under his weight, while his lanky frame made it look as though he was sitting in a child's chair rather than one made for normal-sized human beings.

"Do you have a license plate number for Ms. Clarke's car?" he asked after Athene had given him a description of the girl and a brief timeline of the events of the night in question.

"No. I know it was one of those retro-looking black and gold ones…some kind of vanity thing, I think." She tucked a piece of hair behind her ear, and the garnets in the multiple ear studs she wore glittered in the sunlight coming through the window.

He smiled—the sort of friendly, encouraging smile that would have made my knees a little weak but didn't seem to have much effect on her. "That's helpful. Now, what time did Violet show up?"

"A little after nine-thirty, I think. I know it couldn't have been much earlier than that, because Lucien had already gotten back from speaking to Selena."

At those words, Calvin's gaze flickered back toward me for just a moment. He didn't comment, though, only said, "Was Lucien angry that she'd followed him to Globe?"

"A little, I think." She shrugged. "But then Violet begged him not to be upset with her and said that she'd only come here because she didn't want to be away from him. After that, he seemed to accept the situation. He told her she could actually help him out, because he needed her assistance with a ritual."

"What kind of ritual?"

For the first time, a faint flush appeared on Athene's high cheekbones. "A protection ritual. He wanted it in place before he slept."

I wondered why Lucien would have needed a protection ritual in a place as sleepy and out of the way as Globe. Just a precaution, or was I missing a piece of the puzzle?

"Could you have helped with this ritual?"

Her eyes wouldn't meet his. "Lucien liked to practice sex magic. He said it powered his spells better than anything else. We didn't have that kind of a relationship."

"Ah." Calvin didn't have the kind of complexion that would easily reveal a blush, but I had a feeling he was embarrassed by the direction the conversation had taken. "So, he performed this ritual with Violet."

"Yes."

"And they left after that."

"Yes."

"What time?"

"A little before midnight, I think."

He nodded and wrote a few more notes on the pad he'd brought with him. When he was done, he reached into his pocket and pulled out the medallion he'd fished out of the river earlier that morning. Since it was still encased in a baggie, I had to assume the forensics lab hadn't inspected it yet. Made sense; the place probably wasn't even open on Sundays.

"Do you recognize this?"

Her eyes had widened as soon as he brought it out, which was probably the only confirmation he needed. But Athene nodded and said, "Yes, it's a GLANG medallion."

"Yours?"

She shook her head. "I have one, but I don't wear it much. Mine is still back at my house in Woodland Hills."

I didn't know why her answer surprised me. She was always at Lucien's side, and so I'd just assumed she must also live at his house in Encino.

So much for my assumptions.

"Did Violet have a medallion like this?"

"Yes," Athene replied. "I know Lucien gave her one a couple of months ago. His way of telling her that she was one of his favorites."

Would Lucien have expected me to wear one of those things if I'd given in to him? Probably; I got the feeling he used them as a sort of brand, which was probably part of the reason why Athene didn't wear hers very much. I didn't have any more time to spend on speculation, though, because Calvin went on, "Do you know if she was wearing it when she came to Globe?"

"I—" Athene broke off there, frowning slightly. "I don't remember. It was fairly dark in the house—Lucien doesn't—*didn't*—like to have a lot of lights on. She probably did, though. Once Lucien gave it to her, she always wore the thing."

Calvin made a few more notes. When he was done, he looked back up at Athene. "This evidence is all pretty circumstantial, but I want to ask you anyway. Do you think Violet Clarke murdered Lucien Dumond?"

"No."

Only that one word, but her tone was pretty emphatic. Hazel gave me a quick sideways glance, greenish eyes questioning, and I allowed myself the barest lift of my shoulders. I'd already heard basically the same thing from Athene, but I wondered why Calvin had asked the question. Was he trying to come up with excuses why there was no reason to waste time tracking down Violet when it was obvious she couldn't be the killer?

"Did Lucien have any enemies?"

That question elicited a bitter little chuckle. "Of course he did. All powerful men do. But whether any of them were resourceful enough or strong enough to overpower him? I doubt it." She leaned forward and set down the glass of iced tea she'd been holding the entire time. "That's the problem, Chief Standingbear. I can think of a whole lot of people who would have liked to see Lucien dead, but I can't see how any of them could have managed it. Especially alone and hundreds of miles away from their base of operations."

"But Lucien wasn't exactly operating out of his own backyard."

Athene seemed to consider Calvin's statement for a moment, then shrugged. "No, but he had Violet help him cast a protection spell. That on its own would have been enough to make sure no harm came to him."

Calvin had been impassive through their exchange, expression barely budging, but his mouth twitched then, just the slightest bit. And apparently, Athene had been looking for some sign of disbelief, because she leaned against the back of the sofa, grim satisfaction in her eyes.

"I know you think this all sounds crazy, but it's the truth. Lucien's spells worked just fine. How do you think he's managed to keep himself safe all these years?"

"He didn't keep himself safe Friday night."

Not even a flicker in her heavy-lidded dark eyes. "No, and I think we all want to know the reason why. Since I wasn't there, I can't say for sure." She crossed her arms and stared back at him. "I've told you everything I know. Are you still going to require me to stay in this backwater of yours, or can I go back to L.A.? I have a lot of arrangements to make. I also need to know when Lucien's body will be released."

"You'll have to ask the medical examiner about that," Calvin replied, apparently unperturbed by her "backwater" comment. "I'll give you the number—they'll be open tomorrow morning at eight o'clock."

He flipped over the piece of paper he'd been writing on, then scribbled something on the one beneath it and tore it off. Athene took it from him, mouth tight.

"But sure, you can go back to California," he went on. "Unless, of course, some new evidence presents itself."

Her expression didn't change. "Good. I'll get an airport shuttle set up…unless you found Lucien's car so I can drive it back."

"Haven't found the vehicle yet," Calvin said. "But even if we had, I couldn't release it to you unless you were on the title."

This response seemed to annoy her, although I couldn't tell whether she was irritated more by the fact that the Mercedes was still missing or that she wouldn't have been able to drive it even if it wasn't still MIA.

However, she only replied, "Good to know. Is there anything else?"

Her tone and manner were so imperious, she sounded like a queen dismissing a lackey. Someone else might have taken offense, but

Calvin just said, "No, ma'am. I think that's all for now. I'll be in touch if anything else comes up."

He rose from his chair, nodded at Hazel, and then sent another of those sideways glances at me. A little tingle of anticipation ran down my spine.

Calvin might not have spoken out loud, but that look clearly said, *I'm not done with you yet.*

12

Guess Who's Coming to Dinner

MY WITCHY SIXTH SENSE TOLD ME I NEEDED to get a real dinner together, so after I said goodbye to Hazel and Athene, I headed over to Walmart and got a whole chicken and some fresh veggies, along with what looked like a nice bottle of pinot noir from Washington State. I already had rice on hand, and I figured I'd make a pilaf from the recipe my mother had passed down from my Grandma Ellen.

Some tidying up—and a quick check of my Tarot, the two of cups telling me that yes, playing Suzy Homemaker had been the right call—and a little after six o'clock, the buzzer for the back entrance to the shop sounded.

Perfect.

I hurried downstairs and opened the door.

Calvin Standingbear stood outside, looking diffident.

"Right on time," I told him.

"What?"

"Come on in."

Expression even more nonplussed, he came into the little space that served as the back entrance's foyer. "We need to talk," he said.

"I know," I replied. "Come upstairs. Dinner is almost ready."

"Dinner?"

"You're hungry, aren't you?"

"Well—"

"Exactly."

Without waiting for a reply, I made my way up the stairs. The sound of his quiet, heavy tread told me he'd decided to follow without argument.

When we went inside, the warm aromas of roasting chicken and rice pilaf with almonds greeted us.

"You weren't joking, were you?" Calvin said.

"I never joke about food." Which was only the truth. I didn't know if I could classify myself as a full-on kitchen witch, but I liked to cook and to bake. The soothing routines of following recipes and adding my own personal touches really weren't all that different from performing a ritual or crafting a spell jar, when you got right down to it.

˙ I went into the kitchen and sneaked a peek at the rice. It looked ready to go, fluffy and luscious, and so I turned off the gas and left it to sit with the lid in place. Calvin glanced past me to the table, already set and with the bottle of wine open and airing.

"Please tell me you're not still on duty," I said, noting where his gaze had landed. "I mean, you can't be on duty *all* the time, can you?"

"Technically, I'm off duty," he allowed. "But we have a small department, so I'm still on call if something important comes up."

"Well, a glass of wine won't kill you."

He made an amused sound, not quite a snort, but to my relief, he didn't argue with me. Instead, he asked, "Can I help with anything?"

"We're about ready to go," I replied. "You could get the chicken out of the oven for me, though. The pot holders are in that drawer."

I pointed, and he got out a pair of oven mitts decorated with bees and flowers. They looked so incongruous against his muscular forearms that I wanted to laugh. Somehow, though, I held it together while he knelt down and extricated the roasting pan and the golden-brown bird it held.

"You can set it down on the stovetop," I said, and he put the pan in place on the section of stove not occupied by the pot of pilaf. "And then carve once it's time to eat, because I'm actually terrible at that."

He grinned at my confession, and I sent him over to sit down at the dining table so I could get everything dished up. Within a few minutes, we were both seated and ready to go, candles flickering at the center of the table and from the narrow buffet I used as a sideboard. As I was setting everything up, I'd thought about putting on some soft music to play in the background but had decided against it. I was probably already pushing things enough with the wine.

He'd already poured some pinot noir for both of us, so there wasn't much to do except raise our glasses and clink them against one another.

"You got all this from a psychic flash?" Calvin asked after he took a sip.

"Well, it wasn't *all* a psychic flash," I replied, then sipped some of my wine. Not bad. I didn't really care for white wine with dinner, which was why I'd decided on the pinot noir instead of chardonnay or something. "That stink-eye you were giving me at Hazel's house told me you wanted to talk, so I figured we might as well have our discussion over food."

"It wasn't a stink-eye," he objected, and I tilted my head at him.

"I was on the receiving end of it," I said. "It was totally a stink-eye."

He just shook his head and concentrated for a moment on carving the chicken and laying a lush slice of breast on my plate. Next, he did the same for himself, then cut a small piece off one end. Before he popped it in his mouth, he said, "All right, possibly I was slightly irked that you'd interfered with the investigation again when I expressly told you not to."

I paused. Archie had made himself scarce during my dinner preparations, but that didn't mean he wasn't lurking down the hall, listening to everything Calvin and I said. Actually, for a man in cat form, Archie didn't show much interest in human food. I asked him about it once, and he'd given the cat equivalent of a shrug and told me he didn't want to torture himself with "real" food when there was so little chance of him becoming a human being again any time soon.

Those words had sent a spurt of guilt through me—I knew I hadn't devoted as much time to solving his problem as I probably should have—but I'd only shrugged and said that made some sense, and left it there.

But since Calvin was staring at me, fork in one hand, obviously waiting for me to make some sort of a response, I knew I had to say something.

"Well, I probably wouldn't have done anything, except Josie told me Athene had checked out of her Airbnb—one of Josie's friends owns it—and because I was worried that something might happen to her, I tried checking around. It was just coincidence that she'd ended up renting a room from Hazel. I didn't even know she was thinking about doing that."

As I spoke, though, I remembered Hazel making an off-hand comment about investigating alternative ways of earning some cash, since the money her art brought in tended to be sort of hit or miss. The commission to paint the ceiling of my store had brought in a nice chunk for her, but jobs like that didn't come along all the time, and although her paintings were in galleries all over Arizona, again, those sales weren't what you could call steady income.

But she'd never mentioned renting out her spare room, and so I figured I was telling the truth when I said I had no idea about those plans.

"Hmm," was all Calvin said, which could have meant anything. Or maybe that was his way of letting me know he still wasn't happy about what I'd done, but he also wasn't going to do anything about it.

"Still no sign of Lucien's missing car?" I asked, and he shook his head. Now his expression was resigned, as if he knew he couldn't keep me from talking about the case no matter what he did.

"None," he replied. He lifted his glass of pinot and took a sip. I waited, trying to seem casual, when in reality, I found myself almost mesmerized by the movement of his throat as he swallowed, the faint kiss of wine on his sculpted lips. The guy was seriously distracting. "It's strange, just because a car like that isn't exactly common around here. Also, Mercedes are some of the most difficult cars to break into. It's almost as though whoever took it had their own key fob."

"Couldn't someone, I don't know, have hacked the car's computer?" I seemed to remember reading something like that a while back, although I had to admit that Globe didn't seem like a hotbed of computer-hacking car thieves.

"I suppose it's possible, but it's not very likely." Calvin set down his wine glass. "We'll figure it out eventually."

"What about Violet?"

His shoulders lifted. No uniform this time, only a dark button-up shirt, faded jeans, and scuffed black cowboy boots. I'd already gotten used to the cowboy boots and turquoise jewelry that many of the town's denizens tended to sport, but on him, the boots didn't look silly but downright sexy.

Of course, Calvin could probably manage to look sexy in a pink bunny suit.

He said, "Someone at a gas station on Highway 70 thought they saw a young woman matching her description heading east. I don't

204 · CHRISTINE POPE

know why she'd be going that way—there isn't much out there."

That did sound strange. You'd think if Violet was trying to get out of town, she would have been going in the opposite direction, heading west toward California. "Did she say anything about where she was going?"

Calvin shook his head as he took a bite of rice pilaf. "No. She went inside the convenience store because she paid cash for the gas and bought a bottle of water, but she didn't say much. The attendant remembered her because he thought she seemed young to be driving out there by herself, and also because you don't see many red BMW convertibles around here."

No, that particular part of the world was pretty short on fancy German cars, my own Beetle notwithstanding. It was definitely the land of the pickup—Ford, Chevy, or Dodge—or the SUV, in those same flavors but with some Jeeps thrown in for variety. You'd think a bright blonde nineteen-year-old in a red convertible would stick out like a sore thumb.

If it had been someone else, I might have thought she was headed out to meet up with relatives or friends, but I knew Violet was from Southern California, just like me...or Lucien.

"So...what's next?"

Calvin lifted an eyebrow. "I'll see what the lab

has to say about the medallion—and your knives. They should be released to me by the end of the day tomorrow."

Well, that was something. Not that I'd planned any rituals where I needed the athame, but I didn't like having it and its companion missing from my altar. I had a particular order to the items I placed there, and with two of them gone, it felt like there was a huge hole in that part of my life.

"That's good to hear," I said, and figured I might as well leave it there. "Any other leads?"

"Dinner's great," he said distinctly, and I grinned. Not subtle at all, but I got the point.

"Thanks," I said. "The pilaf's an old family recipe."

"It's delicious." He ate some more, then went on, "I wasn't expecting you to cook for me, but thanks for this."

Oh, I'd love to do a lot more than just cook for him. For the moment, though, I was happy enough to see the way he enjoyed the food. "I like to cook. Usually what I do is make a big batch of something so I can sort of live off that for the week and supplement it with salads or takeout or whatever. Do you cook?"

"Not really. Cops tend to live on takeout. Once a week, my mother sends a care package home with me so I don't starve."

His comment made me wonder why he had that gourmet kitchen if he never really used it. Asking seemed a bit too personal, though, so I decided to let it go for the moment. Anyway, considering how his biceps bulged against his shirt sleeves every time he lifted his fork or reached for his glass of wine, he didn't look as though he was too in danger of starving. And I didn't know why his comment about his mother startled me. After all, I guessed he was probably no more than five years or so older than I, which meant his parents were most likely still around.

"Does your mother live in San Ramon?"

He nodded. "The whole family does. Parents, grandparents, aunts, uncles, cousins...my brothers and sisters, nieces and nephews."

Growing up with just my mother as my family, I'd always wondered what it would be like to be part of such a big clan. "How many brothers and sisters?"

He grinned with a flash of white teeth. "Four. I'm the middle one of five."

Five kids. It was hard for me to imagine being one of so many siblings. I'd had friends in high school who were one of three, and that had seemed like a lot to me. "That must have been fun."

He chuckled and shook his head. "Well, I suppose that depends on your definition of 'fun.'

There was always something going on, that's for sure. My mother might have a different word for it."

"And no one felt like leaving San Ramon?"

For some reason, his expression darkened. However, his tone was light enough as he said, "No, we're tied to this land. It's part of us." He paused, then went on, "I suppose that might be hard for a city girl like you to understand."

I wanted to protest that epithet—I didn't really feel like a city girl—but I knew he was right. Coming from Southern California, I didn't have any real connection to the land…what there was of it, buried under miles and miles of concrete and asphalt. That might have been part of the reason why I hadn't fought too hard against this destiny-driven move to Globe. So much of magical practice had a lot to do with nature, and it was far more difficult to pursue that part of the craft when you had to drive miles to get to any kind of open land. I couldn't even count the beach, since it was always swarming with people and didn't allow any kind of opportunity for quietly communing with nature.

"It sounds nice, actually," I said. "There's not much sense of history in L.A. Everyone seems to be from someplace else."

"And now you're the one from someplace else," he commented, although now he looked slightly amused, as though he wondered what I thought of my current situation.

"I'm not the only one, though," I told him. "I mean, Hazel's from Iowa."

"But she's been here for years."

True. Maybe after you passed some sort of imaginary milestone, you were granted true resident status in Globe. I hoped it wouldn't take seven years, though.

We were both quiet for a little while as we ate our way through our first helpings of food. Calvin asked if I'd like him to carve me another piece of breast, and I said I would. He snagged one of the drumsticks for himself, then said, "How's the shop going?"

"Fine," I replied. "I mean, I've only been open one day, but I got more customers than I thought I would. I might actually break even on this whole gig."

The look he gave me then was deadly serious. "Are you going to be okay?"

Was that actual concern I saw in his expression? I thought it might be. Maybe Archie wasn't the only person in Globe who would be upset if I couldn't stay around.

"Oh, sure," I said lightly. "I can operate in the red for a while since I have a pretty big cushion."

"Even after paying cash for this place?"

I reflected that there didn't seem to be too

many people Josie hadn't blabbed to. But that was all right; while I might have some secrets, my finances weren't one of them. "Even then. I won the lottery back in California."

He'd just swallowed some wine, and seemed to choke a bit as I relayed that piece of information, although he recovered himself quickly enough. "You won the lottery?"

"Yes," I replied. "Not a huge one. I mean, I can't afford a yacht or anything…not that I'd want one. But it's enough to keep me going for a long time even if this shop doesn't make a cent— although obviously, I don't want that to happen. So far, I think it's going to be all right."

For a moment, Calvin was silent, appearing to absorb those latest bits of data. "Do you think that's part of the reason why Lucien came after you?"

"My money?"

"Yes."

"I doubt it," I said frankly. "My little nest egg is peanuts compared to his net worth. His house alone is probably worth at least five or six million."

Surprise flickered in Calvin's eyes. Not for the first time, I noticed the lashes that shaded them, straight and silky and inky black as his hair. That magnificent mane of his was still severely confined to a ponytail, and I had to wonder what it would look like when freed of the leather cord that held it back away from his face.

"I had no idea Lucien had that kind of money."

"Oh, yeah," I said, reaching for my glass of wine.

"Maybe that's why he was murdered."

"For his money?"

Calvin nodded.

I sipped some pinot and pondered his suggestion. Honestly, I didn't know why I hadn't considered that aspect of the situation before this, except that when someone was in Lucien's line of work, you tended to think any foul play had to be supernatural in nature. It wouldn't be the first time someone who'd dabbled in the wrong kind of spells or messed with the wrong entity met a nasty —and untimely—end. Honestly, that made a lot more sense than thinking fragile little Violet Clarke had anything to do with his death.

"Who was Lucien's heir?" Calvin inquired next.

Good question. "I'm not sure," I said slowly. "I mean, Athene was his right-hand woman, so you'd think he'd leave something to her, but I don't know that. He didn't have any children. His parents are still alive, and he has a younger brother, but I don't think they were close."

"Still," Calvin said, "it's a line of inquiry I'd

better look into. Money's often a very powerful motive."

I couldn't argue with that, not when the majority of my clients had wanted me to use my powers of divination to see if their futures would be prosperous, if I could guide them to deals or investments or opportunities that would help fatten their wallets. Of course, I also had many clients who wanted to know about their love lives or their health, but money always seemed to come first.

"Definitely," I agreed. I hesitated for a second, then decided I'd better go ahead and ask the question anyway. "So…am I still a suspect?"

"Do you think I'd be having dinner with you if you were?"

When he put it that way….

Relief spread through me, even as I asked, "Then why are you having the lab check my knives?"

"Because that way I can show I did my due diligence," he said. "It was always a long shot. I can tell you're not a murderer."

"Thanks…I guess."

His eyes crinkled in amusement, and he took a bite of his drumstick before setting it back down. "And I'm not getting that vibe from Athene, either, which is why I told her it was all right to head back to L.A. Of course, with my two main suspects ruled out, that means I'm back to square one."

Yes, that was kind of a problem. But I was glad he hadn't tried to take the easy way out by pinning the murder on the likely suspects—not only because I really didn't want to be arraigned for first-degree murder, but because it also told me Calvin Standingbear was a man with integrity.

After some of my experiences in Los Angeles, that was a welcome change.

Dinner wended down after that. I hadn't had time to bake anything, and so I didn't have much to offer for dessert except some rocky road ice cream I'd bought at Walmart. He declined, saying he wasn't into sweets.

And then came the awkward after-dinner moment as we both got up from the table. Calvin helped me take the dishes into the kitchen, and then we both turned and looked at each other.

"Thanks for dinner," he said. "It was really nice to have some home cooking."

"Any time," I managed. My heart was beating irrationally fast, and I told it to chill out. There was no reason to believe this dinner would end with anything more than a simple goodbye, with maybe a promise that he'd be back to return my knives to me once the lab was done with them.

He paused, gazing down into my face. "You're making this really hard for me," he said.

"I am?"

"I think you know that. In general, I don't have dinner with murder suspects."

"I thought you said I wasn't a suspect."

"True. It's just…." The words trailed off, and he shook his head. "This isn't where I'd intended to be."

"Me, neither," I said. "Globe, that is."

The image of the Lovers card from my Tarot deck flashed into my mind. Back in L.A. when I'd pulled that card, I'd wondered if it meant I had some kind of love life waiting for me in Arizona. Now, with the way Calvin stared down into my face, the intensity in those night-dark eyes of his, I thought maybe the universe was just about to prove to me that, once again, it had been right.

And I was more than fine with that. I'd been waiting longer than I wanted to admit for the right man to cross my path.

Calvin's phone buzzed in his pocket, and he started, backing away from me slightly. "I'll need to take this," he said, tone apologetic but also somehow relieved, as if he was glad of the interruption.

"Sure," I replied, my tone resigned.

Thanks, universe.

He lifted the phone to his ear. "Standingbear here." At once, his expression went almost too still, as if he was trying his best to keep me from

214 • CHRISTINE POPE

guessing what might be passing through his mind. "Yes. Got it. I'll be right there."

Well, he had warned me he was always on call, although I wanted to groan at the timing of this one. If it had come through even a minute later....

"Is something wrong?" I asked.

Calvin nodded, expression stony. "I'm afraid so. That was Ned, one of my deputies. Athene Kappas was just killed in a car crash."

13

The Hand of Fate

LIGHTS FLARED BLUE AND RED ALONG THE steep slopes that rose above Highway 60 as it wound its way out of town to the west. The ambulance was already here, although there was no point in taking poor Athene to the hospital. Her body lay on a gurney behind the ambulance, covered in a sheet, thank the Goddess. To one side stood Travis Cox, Globe's on-and-off-again Uber/Lyft driver.

"I don't know what happened, man," he said. He was a gangly guy maybe ten years older than me, with sandy hair and a scrubby beard and the slightly unfocused gaze of someone who liked to smoke a lot of weed in his spare time. "It's, like, something just grabbed hold of the car and rolled it."

Cold trickled down my spine. I thought once

again of my worries back at the apartment, that something supernatural was at work here, leaving a trail of death in its wake.

Calvin stood next to Chief Lewis, both men clearly not thrilled at the prospect of having to work together. Technically, this stretch of road was in Lewis's jurisdiction, since it lay within Globe's town limits, but because Athene had been part of the investigation into Lucien Dumond's death, Calvin was also involved.

And that meant the two police departments had to work together.

Calvin had brought me along because I begged him. No, I'm not proud of that, but the instant I heard Athene was dead, I knew something hinky had to be going on. Luckily, he agreed that my witchy insights might be of some use, although he warned me to stay out of the way.

"I'm going to tell Lewis that you're there because you're a friend of the victim and her only advocate in town, but you still need to make sure you don't interfere with anything," he said.

I promised I'd behave myself, and that was why I stood off to the side and listened, trying my best to look as inoffensive as possible. Chief Lewis had shot me a gimlet glare as I got out of Calvin's police SUV, but since he hadn't said anything, I figured I'd been given the green light to stay.

"What do you mean, 'something' grabbed

hold of the car?" Lewis asked, clearly displeased by Travis's description of the accident.

"What I said, man." Travis ran a hand through his stringy hair and then crossed his arms. He kept his gaze resolutely away from the still body on the gurney, or the crumpled wreckage of what used to be a Subaru Forester. "Like, I was driving down the highway—doing the speed limit —and then the back wheels started to skid. Next thing I knew, something jerked on the rear end of the car, and we flipped. Rolled two, three times. I can't remember for sure."

"Why wasn't Ms. Kappas wearing her seat-belt?" Calvin asked next.

Because that was why Travis was still standing upright, no worse for wear except a few bumps on his forehead and the beginnings of a laceration from the seat belt visible against the side of his neck, and Athene was on her way to the morgue. When the car rolled, her neck was broken.

Just thinking about it made me slightly queasy.

"I think she dropped her phone," Travis said. "I heard her swear, and I think I saw her bend down to get it but she couldn't reach it. So she undid her seatbelt—and that was when the car started to act weird."

I fought back a shiver. It sure sounded to me as though someone...or something...had put a hex on the car. However, I knew I'd better keep that theory to myself—at least until Calvin and I could talk in private. I didn't even want to think how the hard-jawed Chief Lewis would react if I tried to tell him that Travis's Subaru had been cursed.

Calvin nodded, as if satisfied with the explanation Travis had provided. Lewis, scowled, though, and said, "You been smoking, Travis?"

"No," he replied at once in wounded tones. "Not that I don't have the right," he added, as if he wanted the police chief to understand that he hadn't abstained because of fear of the law. Like California, Arizona had legalized recreational marijuana use, but that didn't mean its residents had a license to drive while high. "But Ms. Kappas had contacted me though the app and let me know she wanted a pickup in a few hours, and so I made sure I was sharp and ready to go."

I had my doubts about how "sharp" Travis was even when he wasn't partaking, but I could tell he wasn't lying. And apparently, Chief Lewis also seemed to accept his story, because he nodded and said, "All right. We'll tow the vehicle in and inspect it, see what kind of mechanical problem caused it to fail like that."

"Wasn't no problem," Travis protested. "I just had a full-on inspection only two months ago.

Brakes, suspension, tires…everything was fine. There's nothing wrong with my car."

"Well, if that's the case, then we won't find anything," Lewis replied. His gaze shifted to Calvin, and I saw his mouth go flat, even as bristles of red flared in his aura. Definitely no love lost there; I had a feeling he griped to his deputies about having to work with an "Injun," even if he was savvy enough not to repeat that kind of thing in mixed company. "You need anything else, Standingbear?"

"I'll take a quick look at the vehicle." Calvin's voice was brisk, no-nonsense, although he sounded friendly enough as he directed his next words to Travis. "You need a lift home, Travis?"

"If you could," the other man said. From his obvious relief, I could tell he was much happier getting a lift from Calvin than from Chief Lewis.

Not that I could blame him.

"Sure thing," Calvin said, and clapped Travis on the shoulder. "Just give me a few minutes, and then I'll get you out of here."

Travis shot him a relieved glance, then headed over to a large boulder on the side of the highway. He leaned up against it, hands jammed in his pockets, and stared, mouth drooping, at the wreckage of his vehicle.

Calvin walked over to me and said in an undertone, "You getting anything from all this?"

"You mean like what I felt down by the river?" I replied in a similar murmur.

He nodded. Across the way, Chief Lewis stared at us with narrowed eyes, but then his shoulders lifted, and he walked back over to his deputy, who'd been standing guard by the gurney next to an EMT the whole time. They shared a few words, and then the EMT and the deputy hefted the gurney into the back of the ambulance.

The slam of its doors seemed far too loud, and I jumped. Calvin gave me a sympathetic glance.

"Hell of a first date."

"Is that what it was?"

A corner of his mouth lifted slightly. "Maybe. Can you come with me to Travis's car?"

"Sure."

I told myself I shouldn't be feeling so happy, not when Athene Kappas lay dead a few yards away from me in the back of an ambulance. And maybe "happy" wasn't even the correct word for the way I felt right then.

Excited…hopeful.

Calvin had called our dinner a date, not me.

We walked over to the wreckage of Travis's Subaru. It had been pushed mostly onto the shoulder; flares surrounded it, letting passing motorists know to give the spot a wide berth. Not that there was probably much traffic coming and going on Highway 60 on a Sunday night, thankfully.

The car wasn't brand-new, but it looked as though Travis did a good job of maintaining it, because the paint that wasn't scratched and scraped looked clean, and the tires appeared fairly new as well. I felt a stab of pity for the poor thing ending up like this, because even my unpracticed eyes could tell the frame had been bent and the vehicle was totaled.

I didn't think I made any kind of sound, but Calvin must have picked up something because he said, "Travis's insurance will take care of most of it. He had to have it fully insured to be driving for Uber."

"What about the deductible?" Somehow, I doubted Travis had an extra thousand bucks—or even five hundred—lying around to cover that sort of expense.

Calvin looked as though he wanted to reach out and give me a reassuring pat on the arm. Since we had something of an audience—Chief Lewis and his deputy still loitered on the scene, probably waiting for the tow truck to arrive—he just said, "Then Josie will organize some kind of a fundraiser. They do that in Globe. Take care of their own, I mean."

Even though I was new to town and probably wouldn't be classified as one of "their own"…at least not yet…I couldn't help but be relieved by Calvin's words. It felt good to be in a place where people looked out for each other.

"That's good to hear," I said.

"Not much like L.A., I'm guessing."

"Not a lot, no." It wasn't that people didn't try to look out for one another when they could, but just being neighbors usually wasn't enough of an incentive to get involved the way it obviously was in this particular small town.

Far down the highway appeared a set of flashing lights, getting closer. Calvin glanced over at them and frowned.

"The tow truck," he said briefly. "We need to get on this."

The way he said "we" heartened me, although at the same time, I couldn't help experiencing just a twinge of worry. It seemed as if he now wanted to include me as an informal member of his team.

I had to hope I wouldn't disappoint him.

As he walked around the vehicle, snapping a series of images with his phone, I stayed off to one side. The strobing lights from the ambulance and the various cop cars didn't do much to help my concentration, although I tried to ignore them as best I could.

I had to focus.

At first, I didn't feel anything at all, except a certain jangly energy I guessed came from Calvin and probably Travis, who stood only a few yards away from us. Beneath that, though, there came a dark, creeping sensation, sort of like the world's worst goosebumps marching a parade down my spine.

Without thinking, I stepped forward and placed a hand on the Subaru's mangled bumper. A shock of cold went up my arm, and I gasped and jumped back.

Immediately, Calvin looked over at me, phone idle in his hand. "You okay, Selena?"

I shook my head. "No," I said, then hurriedly added as he began to frown, "I mean, *I'm* fine. But there's something very wrong here. I don't practice this kind of thing, so I don't know exactly what went down with the car, but it definitely feels as if it was tampered with somehow."

"'Tampered with'?" he repeated. "You mean like cutting the brake lines or something?"

"Worse than that," I told him. "Dark magic… a hex, I guess."

Although his expression didn't change, I could almost feel the way his body stiffened. He might have said he was willing to believe in all sorts of things, but when I came right out and started talking about hexes and dark magic, that was a whole other story.

To my relief, though, he didn't try to contradict me. "You're sure?"

"'Sure' is a strong word," I said. "Magic isn't science. It's kind of the antithesis of science. All I can do is tell you how it feels to me."

"Your instincts have been pretty good so far."

Maybe. If they'd been really good, I would have sensed a dark cloud hanging over Athene…I would have had the foresight to tell her that driving off with Travis was a really bad idea.

Except if there actually was a hex on his car, that meant someone had been determined to get her no matter what the collateral damage. And if that was really the case, then it probably didn't matter which way she'd tried to get out of town… any attempt at leaving would have been doomed to failure.

The chill that went over me right then didn't have much to do with the dark magic I'd sensed on Travis's Subaru…or the cold night air. The days had started to warm, but Globe still got downright chilly overnight.

Who would want Athene Kappas dead so badly, it didn't matter who else got in the way?

Some people might have argued that because she worked so closely with Lucien, his enemies were her enemies. For all I knew, that was the simple truth. But….

Calvin stepped closer to me as he slipped his phone back into his pocket. His voice was calm as he said, "You don't have to try to solve this tonight. We need to get Travis home."

"What if the killer is already moving on to his next victim?" I asked. "What if that next victim is me?"

For a moment, he didn't reply, only stared at the crumpled Subaru with unreadable dark eyes. Then he replied, "I don't think that's too likely. Athene was very closely connected to Lucien Dumond. Horrible as her death is, it at least makes some sense when you look at the situation that way. You've made it pretty clear you didn't want anything to do with him, so I don't know why someone would target you."

I wanted to believe him. He sounded so calm, so plausible. I told myself that I was understandably freaked out. After all, I'd never been connected to a murder before, let alone multiple murders. And I'd talked to Athene earlier that day. She'd seemed shaken but otherwise all right. It was hard to believe she was gone.

And yes, I believed—well, actually, I *knew,* thanks to communicating with my departed grandmother—that death on this plane, in this life, wasn't the end. Athene had moved on. *Truly* moved on, I thought, since I hadn't felt a hint of her presence at the accident scene. No lingering dregs of fear and pain like there had been down by the San Ramon River. Her end might have been a violent one, but it hadn't consigned her to an eternity of haunting this lonely stretch of Highway 60.

"You're probably right," I said. "Let's take Travis home."

Travis lived in a shabby little bungalow on one of Globe's hillier streets, in a neighborhood that reminded me somehow of San Francisco—probably because of the steep hillsides and the collection of last turn-of-the-century homes that clustered there. Of course, in San Francisco, even Travis's tiny house would have been worth more than a million, while I doubted in Globe it would go for a tenth of that.

He got out of the Durango's back seat, thanked Calvin, and headed up the front walk, looking pretty spry for someone whose car had just flipped a few times. Then again, he was probably hurrying so he could get inside and smoke a bowl for his aches and pains. If I'd been in his shoes, I would've been thinking the same thing.

Calvin pointed the SUV back toward downtown so he could take me home. As he pulled up next to my Volkswagen at the back of the store, he said, "You sure you're going to be all right?"

Part of me wanted to say no, I wouldn't, just

to see whether he'd offer to sleep on my couch and keep watch all night. But I held my tongue. I didn't want to make him think I couldn't look after myself…even as I wondered whether I would be up to the task.

He walked me to the back door and watched as I let myself in, but his manner seemed almost oddly formal. Most likely, he'd realized it was the wine talking earlier and nothing more, and was now probably grateful for the phone call that had interrupted him before he did something really stupid.

"Call me if you see or hear anything that seems off," he said.

"It'll be fine," I replied, even as I wondered if it really would be. Two people dead in the span of forty-eight hours. Who else would be next?

His mouth tightened. "I hope so. But I mean it. Don't hesitate—just call if you feel even a little weird about something."

I wanted to tell him that I was already feeling pretty weird. But hinkiness wasn't enough of an excuse to ask him to stay and babysit me, so I just nodded. However, I couldn't quite keep myself from slanting a sideways glance up at him as I asked, "Shouldn't I be calling Globe P.D. if some-thing really does go down? This isn't even your jurisdiction."

If anything, his lips compressed even further.

"I'm not sure the Barney Fifes are up to this sort of thing."

Despite everything, I couldn't help chuckling. Globe's deputies were probably okay if called on to handle a traffic accident or a burglary or maybe even a domestic dispute, but I had to admit that they weren't quite up to the task of handling some kind of supernatural serial murderer.

If that was even what we were up against. I almost wanted to tell myself that I'd been imagining things back at the accident scene, that the feelings of cold and dread I'd experienced were my own fear and unease talking, but I couldn't quite convince myself of that. Something strange was definitely going on, even if I couldn't quite identify what it might be.

"You have a point," I said lightly. "Okay, I'll call. But I'm sure everything will be quiet. Like you said, I'm only tangentially connected to all this."

Calvin nodded. "Right. Take care—and turn on your alarm system."

Because of course he'd noticed it when he came over for dinner. Alison Carruthers, the woman who'd renovated the property, had installed the alarm, although at the time, I'd found myself wondering if such measures were really necessary in sleepy little Globe. Now, though, I was damn glad of having a security system, even if I didn't know for sure how much good it would do to ward off hexes and dark magic.

"I will." I paused, then said, "Thanks for taking me along with you. I don't think Chief Lewis was too thrilled about it, though."

The grim look left Calvin's mouth, and he actually appeared halfway amused. "Maybe someday I'll tell you how much I don't care about Chief Lewis's opinion."

I couldn't help smiling. "Good to know—and good night."

Still wearing that smile, I let myself in, then locked the door behind me and engaged the alarm system. I hadn't turned it on when we left, mostly because Calvin and I had been in such a hurry.

It actually did give me a spurious sense of safety, although that sense only lasted until I heard Calvin's SUV backing away from the building and moving down the alleyway that separated my place from the empty lot behind it. My smile disappeared as well.

Damn, I really wished I hadn't been such a coward about asking him to stay.

I mounted the stairs to find Archie sitting in the entry of my apartment, tail flicking back and forth in irritation. "Are you going to come and go at such odd hours every time that man visits you?"

Considering this was only the second time

Calvin had come over to my apartment, I thought Archie was being a bit melodramatic. "I don't know," I said. "But a woman I know died in a car accident tonight, so I'd appreciate you showing a little respect."

For Archie, he looked almost ashamed. Or at least, he ducked his head and pretended to rub it against his foreleg, as if he didn't quite know how to react to such a statement. "I'm sorry to hear that."

I doubt it, I thought, but I decided it was better not to push things. If nothing else, he was pretending to be shamefaced, and I figured that was a start. As for the rest....

"You're actually lucky we had to go out," I remarked. "Otherwise, I don't know where things might have been headed."

That vague allusion was enough to make his eyes flare wide in alarm. "You wouldn't."

"This is my house, Archie," I told him. "If I want to do the horizontal hokey-pokey with the world's hottest chief of police, that's my prerogative. You can go hide under the dining room table or something while we're doing the deed."

His tail whipped back and forth. "Just let me out before you get started," he shot back. "I'll make sure to stay far, far away."

"It's a deal," I said. "Anything else? It's late, and I'm tired."

"No," he replied. "I think that is all."

"Good."

Without waiting to see if he wanted to respond, I headed into the bedroom and shut the door, glad that the apartment had been renovated with an *en suite* bathroom so I wouldn't have to emerge again that night. I kicked off my shoes and removed my jewelry, placing it in the little hand-made ceramic dish I'd bought at a street fair in Santa Monica years ago.

I hadn't been lying to Archie when I'd said I was tired. Exhausted, actually, even though I realized when I glanced over at the clock on my bedside table that it really wasn't all that late. A little past ten, no more, and I often stayed up past midnight, especially if I needed to perform a moon ritual or set out my crystals to recharge at a particular time.

But the moon was waning, and I didn't have plans for any more rituals until the new moon on April twenty-second, not quite two weeks away.

Problem was, when I laid my head on the pillows and closed my eyes, my brain didn't seem to have gotten the memo that my body was ready to get some rest. Instead, my thoughts kept racing, trying to find patterns where none seemed to have yet emerged.

I didn't find it too hard to believe that Lucien had driven someone to murder, but why Athene?

Was this unknown killer a person who thought himself so wronged by the former head of GLANG that he couldn't be content with just getting rid of the man in charge, but had to murder Lucien's right-hand woman as well?

And all right, I knew I was mentally assigning a gender to this unknown killer when no one knew who he—or she—really was. I supposed the murders could have been committed by a woman, but I didn't think so. My instincts were telling me otherwise.

Great. So now I'd narrowed the suspect down to a little less than half the planet's population.

I rolled over on my side and stared moodily at the faint glow of the streetlights beyond the blinds. In the past, the light had never bothered me, because it certainly wasn't bright enough to really disturb my sleep. That night, though, it seemed as if not much was required to keep me awake.

All right. I told my brain that a tired and cranky witch wasn't an effective witch, but those inner admonitions didn't seem to help much. Letting out a sigh, I shifted onto my back again, figuring I usually fell asleep that way, so I might as well increase the odds.

And what was going on with Violet Clarke? I couldn't imagine her as a cold-blooded killer—especially not one as powerful as the magical residue at the crash site seemed to indicate—but she wasn't exactly acting like an innocent party, either. I wished I'd pressed Athene to tell me more about what Violet had said when she showed up in Globe. But since the subject had obviously been a sore one, I'd decided to let it go…and now I had very little to work with.

As I stared up at the ceiling, I tried to catalog the other magical practitioners in the greater Los Angeles area, doing my best to determine whether any of them might be behind this whole mess. None of them seemed powerful enough, though —or motivated enough. I wouldn't say that any of us had really liked Lucien, but neither had we harbored the kind of animus that would result in murder. Pretty much everyone—myself included —had done what we could to stay out of his orbit.

You don't have to solve this tonight, I told myself, my inner voice doing its best to sound reassuring.

I wasn't reassured, though.

Who knew what might happen while I was asleep?

14

Stones and Spirits

As far as I could tell, no catastrophes had occurred overnight. Because it was Monday and the shop was technically supposed to open at eleven, I dutifully got out of bed and went through my morning routine—coffee and yogurt and yoga—then pulled my one card for the day from my crow Tarot deck.

Two of wands.

Clearly, I needed to make a plan of action. I just wasn't sure what that plan was supposed to be.

Well, first things first.

After showering and getting dressed, I headed down to the store, even though it was only a little past ten and I had some time before my "official" opening. However, I'd already learned that people operated on their own schedules in Globe, and if I wanted to get an early start to my day, why not?

Just like the day before, the sun shone down brightly on that particular corner of Arizona. Probably on the whole state; Josie had told me how summers could often be cloudy and turbulent there, with spectacular monsoon thunderstorms, but those days were still months off.

It didn't feel quite right that the day should look so cheerful when people appeared to be dying right and left, but I knew the weather often had very little to do with what was actually going on in people's lives.

Or deaths.

I really wasn't expecting many customers on a Monday, and so I was surprised when Fiona O'Neil, a crony of Josie's, popped in almost as soon as I opened my doors. She was as slender as Josie was plump, with gorgeous thick white hair she always wore back in a smooth ponytail.

"Hi, Fiona," I said politely. "Can I help you with something?"

"That citrine cluster," she replied, pointing to the impressive chunk of rock that had a place of honor inside the locked glass case that contained my showiest—and most expensive—specimens.

"Sure," I said. "Just let me get the key."

I retrieved the key to the case from its place beneath the cash register, then opened the sliding door on the back of the display. The chunk of citrine was heavy, weighing almost eight pounds, and so I had to use both hands to extract it from its spot on the shelf and set it on top of the case.

"Is it all right if I touch it?" Fiona asked.

"Of course," I told her. "You need to be able to feel its energy."

An embarrassed little flush rose in her cheeks. "Is that—is that *really* a thing? Feeling vibrations off crystals, or whatever?"

"It's definitely a thing," I responded. "People react to different stones in different ways. But citrine is known for its positive energy. It also can help to attract financial success and wealth."

"Oh, really?" She put her hands around the chunk, fingers lightly resting on its myriad points. "I suppose that can only be a good thing. I just know I saw it in the case at your opening on Friday night and thought it was beautiful. And then I kept thinking about it all weekend…."

"Well, if you couldn't get it out of your mind, that means you connected with it," I said. "I think stones know who they're supposed to be with."

Her expression turned half hopeful, half skeptical, as if she wanted to believe me but didn't know whether she should. "Really?"

"Really," I echoed. "I have this gorgeous—and huge—piece of quartz I got from a mineral show a year ago. The minute I touched it, I knew it needed to go home with me. I didn't know if I could justify the expense, but I went ahead and bought it. And ever since then, I've had really good luck."

Like having Lucien Dumond gunning for you? passed through my mind, although I squelched the thought as quickly as I could. Everything happened for a reason, even if we couldn't always see the pattern at first. I had to believe that the universe wanted me in Globe. Whether that was so I could hook up with Calvin Standingbear, or so I'd be in the right place at the right time to solve Lucien's murder...or even just so I could open my shop and dispense metaphysical advice to the town's residents...I couldn't say for sure.

Maybe all of the above.

"I'll take it," Fiona said. She spoke quickly, as if she knew she needed to lay claim to the stone before she changed her mind.

"Wonderful," I said. "Let me wrap it up for you. Credit card?"

Since the chunk of citrine was nearly three hundred dollars, I sort of doubted she would pay me in cash. And she did hand over her card, although it was a platinum debit one and not an actual credit card.

Even better. I didn't like the thought of people going into debt to purchase the pieces they wanted.

I processed the transaction, then got out

several sheets of brown wrapping paper and did my best to make sure the citrine would get home safely. After carefully placing it in a heavy-duty gift bag, I set it on the counter.

"Here you go," I told her. "I hope you enjoy it."

"Oh, I will," Fiona replied. "I have the perfect spot for it picked out on my mantel."

She went out after that, carrying the bag in both hands so there was no chance of the bottom ripping out. I watched her go, feeling oddly happy. And no, it wasn't just that I'd managed to sell one of the most expensive pieces in my shop. It was more that I knew the citrine had gone exactly where it was supposed to go. Also, Fiona's husband was a manager at the Fairport mining company, which still operated a huge plant on the outskirts of Globe. I knew she probably hadn't even put a dent in her discretionary spending for the month with the purchase, so I could bask in the afterglow of the sale guilt-free.

Unfortunately, that afterglow didn't last very long. About fifteen minutes after Fiona left—and just a little after eleven, the time the shop was officially supposed to open—Chief Lewis came through the front door, wearing the scowl that seemed to be perpetually fixed on his hard features.

Or maybe that was just the expression he always wore whenever in my presence.

"Good morning," I said politely. "Looking for something in particular? Incense? Essential oils?"

He managed to look even more annoyed, if that was possible. "Tell me what you were doing at the crash site last night."

"Calvin asked me to come with him, since I knew the victim," I replied.

His eyes went from flinty to positively glacial. Maybe it was the way I'd referred to Calvin so casually, or maybe it was simply that he didn't like being reminded that the chief of the tribal police had just as much jurisdiction in the matter, if not more. "Are you a detective, Ms. Marx?" he rasped. "A police officer?"

"No," I said sweetly. It was a lovely morning and I'd just made a huge sale, so I refused to let him put me off my stride. "But I am a psychic."

He sniffed. "So you say."

"It's more than just 'saying,' Chief Lewis," I told him, picking up exactly why he seemed to be in an even more foul temper than usual. "You're in a bad mood because you forgot it was your wife's birthday and she read you the riot act before you left for work this morning."

His hard gray eyes widened, flickering with disbelief before the familiar scowl clamped back down again. "Josie must have told you that."

"No," I said. "Actually, I haven't even seen her today. And there's no reason to get that information from her, because I can feel it coming off you in waves. Maybe you should try to make it up to your wife by getting her a nice present. I have lots of lovely jewelry in the case here."

"Becky isn't into all this woo-woo stuff," he retorted. Actually, he practically snarled the words, nostrils flaring in dislike.

"A lot of the jewelry isn't 'woo-woo,'" I replied calmly. "They're items I chose because they're beautiful. What about that amethyst pendant down there?" I pointed at a really lovely piece, a stylized square cross set with faceted amethysts and smooth moonstone cabochons, with delicate Bali-style beadwork on the sections between the bezels. "Purple's her favorite color, isn't it?"

He stared at the pendant, brow still creased with a frown. "It's a cross. I thought you types weren't Christian."

"I'm not," I said, doing my best to keep my voice as neutral as possible. "Or rather, I believe there's something of value to be found in all the world's religions. Jesus was a follower of the light, like many others. So, why wouldn't I have a cross in my store?"

Obviously, such a confounding thought had never crossed Chief Lewis's mind. He continued to stare down at the pendant in the case, almost as if that was easier because at least that way, he wouldn't have to meet my eyes. At last, in grudging tones, "How much?"

"Seventy-five dollars," I replied. "And I can wrap it up and put it in a nice gift box for you."

Another long pause. "All right."

Trying not to smile, I pulled the pendant out of the case, then busied myself with wrapping it up in some of the silvery paper with little white stars blazoned on it that I'd bought exactly for occasions such as this one. I topped it with a neat white bow, and slid it across the top of the display case toward the chief.

He got out his wallet and put down five twenty-dollar bills. Trying to hide from his wife exactly how much he'd spent on her birthday gift?

Maybe.

That wasn't any of my business, though. I picked up the twenties and counted out the change for him. He took it without comment, and also picked up the gift box and stuck it in the pocket of his jacket. Why he was still wearing it when the day promised to be just as mild as the one before, I had no idea.

Again, none of my business.

"You still need to stay out of the Dumond case," he said next. Clearly, even if I'd thought the matter was dropped, he hadn't.

Count to three, I told myself. The number

three had a myriad of magical meanings, although in this context, its significance mostly lay in its ability to keep me from tearing the police chief a new one.

"I'd say that was up to Chief Standingbear," I replied, figuring I might as well not antagonize Lewis even more by referring to Calvin by his first name. "The case is in his jurisdiction, isn't it?"

"The *original* murder," Chief Lewis allowed, although he didn't look very happy about having to admit even that much. "But Floyd's accident happened in Globe's town limits, which means it happened on my beat."

"Have you found out anything from inspecting the vehicle?"

The frown returned, and I had a feeling I wouldn't be able to distract him with a gift for his wife this time. "Like I said, Ms. Marx…stay out of it."

"No worries," I said sweetly. "I'm sure Calvin will tell me when he has a chance."

So much for trying to maintain our fragile truce.

Chief Lewis didn't take the bait. His hand touched the pocket that held his wife's present, as though to reassure himself it was still there. Voice even, he said, "Have a good day, Ms. Marx."

He headed out, spine as straight as if he was

on review back in the Marines. I watched him go, smiling faintly.

If nothing else, I'd made another sale.

The rest of the day was fairly quiet. A few more tourists wandered through, and bought some small crystals and a couple of books. Nothing huge, but it was a very good day for a Monday.

Still, the image of the Tarot card I'd pulled that morning still danced in my brain. The two of wands signified forward movement, which meant I needed to come up with a plan of action. Making a couple of good sales didn't seem quite significant enough.

Then what?

I saw sunlight dancing off the surface of the San Ramon River. Green leaves rustling in the breeze.

Was I supposed to go back there?

Possibly. After all, I hadn't gotten very far with my investigations before Calvin appeared and I went straight into the drink. Everything had been so crazy busy since then, I hadn't really thought about returning.

But if Lucien's spirit lingered there...if there was even a chance I could get him to talk, to tell me who had done this to him...then I needed to go.

I glanced up at the clock I'd hung on the wall above the counter. Ten minutes after four. Since I'd opened early, I figured it couldn't hurt if I closed a little early. No one had been in for the past half hour, so I doubted I'd be disappointing any last-minute shoppers.

Before I even realized what they were doing, my feet propelled me over to the door so I could shut it and lock it, and then hang up the little "Be Back at" sign. Afterward, I hurried upstairs to get into jeans and my hiking boots—now at last completely dry—and then just as quickly went back down to get into my car.

Because it was such a gorgeous day, I put the top down. I kept a collection of scrunchies in the glove compartment for just these sorts of occasions, and I reached in and grabbed a teal blue one to go with my top.

As I drove, I wondered if I should text Calvin and let him know what I was doing. He'd been pretty radio-silent all day, and I didn't quite know what to make of that. I supposed he could have simply been extremely busy, and since I hadn't reached out to him with any problems or concerns, he'd decided to allow some space between us.

This scenario seemed plausible enough, even if

I didn't much like it. *Anyway,* I told myself, *he interrupted you last time. Maybe his energy isn't the best thing to have around when you're trying to reach out to Lucien.*

Especially since I would never have allowed Lucien in my pants, whereas I'd be more than happy to grant Calvin that same access...after we'd gotten to know each other a bit better, of course.

Having rationalized away any reason to reach out to him, I continued to the parking area where I'd first left the Volkswagen. Yes, maybe it would have been better to keep going on the Forest Service road that went a lot closer to the actual spot where Lucien had died, but my instincts were telling me that wasn't such a good idea. I supposed it was possible that impulse stemmed from a desire to avoid doing any more damage to my car's suspension rather than any concrete reasons for heading there, although I told myself that I'd sensed the residue of Lucien's death after making my way along the river bank, so I might as well follow the same path now.

I parked my car and got out, then headed down to the river. It was maybe a bit warmer than it had been the first time I'd come this way, but otherwise, I might have been experiencing a very extended, very vivid *déjà vu.* The same cotton-wood trees cast dappled patterns of light and shadows on the ground, and the San Ramon made the same rustling sounds as its water flowed over the rocks that made up its bed.

This time, though, I'd remembered to bring a bottle of water with me. I broke the seal on the lid and swallowed some before I began walking along the bank, following the path the river cut through the landscape. From overhead came a keening cry, and I flinched for a moment before I realized the sound had probably come from a red-tail hawk and not Lucien Dumond's disembodied spirit.

My heart still beat a little faster than it should as I picked my way over the stony ground. I'd brought my pendulum with me, although it remained in my jeans pocket for the moment, since I already knew where I was going. Shoved in another pocket were a couple of chunks of black tourmaline, my go-to for protecting myself from bad energy. Its presence might keep Lucien's spirit away entirely, but I had to hope that his desire to be heard would overcome the stones' repelling properties.

In life, he'd certainly liked the sound of his own voice.

After a few minutes of picking my way along the rock-strewn riverbank, I came to the small sandy beach where I was almost positive Lucien had been murdered. The same footprints marred the sand, although blurrier now, as if the breezes of the past few days had begun to erase all those traces of human activity.

It was very quiet, with even the sound of the river flowing over its stones somehow muted. I'd worked up something of a sweat during my mini-hike to get here, but I still was cold, a chill inching its way down my spine.

No matter how beautiful the place was, I couldn't quite forget that a man had died in this very spot.

I reached in my pocket with my free hand and touched one of the black tourmalines. It didn't feel hot, which reassured me a little. If it had already gone to work repelling whatever negative energies lurked in my immediate surroundings, it would have been warm to the touch, if not down-right scorching.

All right, then. A few days had passed, and so it was possible that Lucien's spirit had come to terms with its untimely demise and had decided to move on, to jump back on the wheel of life and be spun into a new existence…with any luck, one where he might learn a bit more about how not to be an utter jerk.

But I wasn't here to ponder what karma had in store for him. No, I just needed to find out if he was still around, and, if so, whether he could give me any useful information.

I wasn't a medium; my only real experience

speaking with the dead had been communicating with the ghost of my Grandma Ellen during our sessions with a crystal ball. Despite that lack, I figured I was a little bit ahead of the general population when it came to dealing with spirits, if for no other reason than I at least believed such a thing was possible.

In the same pocket as my pendulum rested my favorite piece of quartz, a beautiful little point with just the faintest veiling within. Like the much larger chunk of quartz I'd told Fiona about, this piece also resonated with me on a very deep level, allowing me to both focus within and at the same time allow my consciousness to open up to higher entities.

Or, in this case, Lucien Dumond.

I set my water bottle down on a large, flat rock nearby, then took out the piece of quartz and wrapped both my hands around it. The energy from the stone shimmered along my nerve endings, letting me know I was open to all vibrations.

"Lucien?" I said aloud. Not too loud, though. A spirit was everywhere; no need to shout.

An odd little breeze caught at the end of my hair, still confined to its scrunchie. In fact, it felt almost like a tug.

I forced myself to remain motionless. I'd been in places before where spirits were active, and so this wasn't exactly my first rodeo. Then again, none of those spirits had been the ghosts of people I actually knew.

"Are you there?"

Again that tug, this time forceful enough that I couldn't help wincing.

"Okay, good," I said, trying to sound calm and reassuring. "Can you speak?"

The wind whispered past my face. "*Selena....*"

I'd always liked my name, even though the only reason my mother had picked it out for me was because she'd thought I'd be a Cancer—aka Moon Child, the sign whose ruling planet was the moon—since my projected arrival was supposed to be on June thirtieth. But I'd jumped the gun and come nine days early, and had turned out to be a Gemini instead. Since she didn't have a backup name, she'd stuck with Selena.

Anyway, I'd liked having a pretty, unusual name. Hearing it whispered on the wind like that, however, was enough to make the hair on the back of my neck stand up.

"I'm here to help," I said. "Can you tell me what happened to you?"

The same rage and fear I'd felt earlier returned, only tenfold. I shuddered and almost lost my balance. Damn it, even as a spirit, he was *strong*.

"Something terrible, I know." As I spoke, I tried to keep my voice calm, persuasive. "We all want to find justice for you, Lucien. We need to know who did this to you."

This time, the wind that blew past me was so fierce, it pulled the scrunchie from my hair and sent it spinning into the water. The loosened strands whipped around my face, bringing tears to my eyes. I blinked, doing my best to focus on the now-blurred scene in front of me.

"*Vile,*" a voice whispered.

Lucien's voice.

"Yes, it was vile," I said. "But I need to know who did this to you."

A tree branch broke off with a sharp *crack* and fell to the ground. I winced, even though the bough had landed a few yards away from me and didn't present any immediate danger.

"*Sheeeeee….*" the voice said. Now it sounded like a low rumble, much deeper than Lucien's voice when he'd still been alive. It reverberated in my eardrums, and I shook my head, even though that didn't do much to clear the painful throbbing.

"I don't understand," I said, even as I began to wonder whether this had been such a great idea after all. I could tell he was trying to communicate, but it just wasn't getting through.

"*Vile!*" the voice shouted, almost in my ear.

"Yes, I got that the first time," I snapped, although I knew that losing my temper wasn't the best way to deal with the situation. So much could be lost in translation when spirits were trying to reach through the veil and communicate. This wasn't the same as having a cozy chat with my grandmother's ghost through the medium of a crystal ball. No, this was facing the raw power of an angry, vengeful spirit, one that couldn't quite form the necessary words to give me the answers I needed.

Still, I had to try.

Then Lucien said, "*Huge*," and I only frowned again.

"What's huge?" I asked. "Was there some kind of conspiracy going on? Was more than one person involved in your death?"

"*HUGE!*" the spirit bellowed again, and I clapped my hands over my ears. That last blast had been so loud, I felt as though I was back in high school and standing too close to the speakers at one of my school dances.

Not helping, I thought grimly. However, the additional decibels seemed to tell me that I might be on the right track. There had been an additional level of intensity in that last reply, as though I'd struck a nerve.

My phone chose that inopportune time to start ringing. At once, the wild wind whistling across the little beach died away. Although he'd never manifested physically, and therefore I couldn't see for sure that Lucien was gone, I somehow knew he'd disappeared.

"Damn it," I muttered under my breath. I pushed my hair out of my face and pulled the phone out of my pocket so I could look at the screen.

Calvin.

Under other circumstances, I would have been happy to have him calling me out of the blue. Right then, however, I was more irritated than anything else.

"What?" I said as I swiped across the screen to accept the call.

"Did I interrupt something?"

I hesitated. Most likely, Calvin wouldn't be too thrilled to learn I'd come back to the murder scene on my own…especially after what had happened to Athene the night before. "Not really," I lied. "What's up?"

"I got your knives back from the lab, so I thought I'd bring them over."

Talk about timing. While I wanted my knives returned safely to their altar, I couldn't quite help cursing the universe for causing such an interruption when I'd been so close to a breakthrough.

Okay, maybe not *that* close. But I'd gotten Lucien talking, which was something.

"Um…I'm running an errand right now. But I

can meet you at my apartment in about twenty minutes."

Maybe a brief hesitation, as if he was attempting to figure out whether I was being entirely truthful. But then he said, "Sure, that'll work. I'll see you then."

He hung up, and I slipped my phone back into my pocket. No choice now except to head home and accept the return of my knives with as good grace as possible.

Before I left, though, I closed my eyes and tried to reach out with that extra sense of mine, the one that had come to my aid so many times before.

Nothing. Or at least, nothing beyond the vibrant life in the trees and the river, the slow strength of the earth beneath my feet. Lucien might have been here a few minutes earlier, but he was certainly gone now.

I let out a sigh and began to trudge back to my car.

15

Spells and Stories

I BARELY HAD TIME TO TAKE OFF MY HIKING
boots and slide into a pair of flats—because one
look at those boots, and Calvin would know I'd
been up to no good—before the buzzer at the
back entrance to the building sounded. A quick
pass of a brush through my hair, and then I
hurried downstairs to open the door.

"Hi," I said, trying not to sound too breath-
less. "Come on in."

Apparently, I wasn't terribly convincing,
because he cocked an eyebrow at me. To my relief,
though, he only said, "Sure," and followed me
upstairs to the apartment.

He carried a baggie with the two knives
inside, and set it down on the dining room table
once we were in my apartment. "Here you go," he
said. "Forensics didn't find anything."

"I told you they wouldn't."

"I know. But the 'I's have been dotted and the 'T's crossed, so now I can say I did my due diligence."

Meaning…what? That he now thought it was safe to date me, as he'd hinted the other evening?

"Well, that's something." I glanced down at the baggie that held my knives, but I didn't bother to pick it up. Before I could use them again, I'd have to make sure they were cleansed and recharged. The Goddess only knew what kind of weird energy they'd picked up at the police station.

Calvin followed my gaze, and a small frown puckered his eyebrows. Maybe he was wondering why I hadn't gone ahead and taken the knives back into the room that held my altar. His next question was one I'd halfway been expecting.

"Are you going to tell me where you were when I called?"

For someone who wasn't psychic, he had good instincts. Too good, actually.

I'd lied on the phone, but I didn't have the guts to lie to his face.

No, it was something more than that. I didn't want to lie to him at all.

"I was down at the river."

At once, his frown deepened. Voice full of warning, he began, "Selena—"

"I know," I cut in. Maybe I'd earned a scolding, but I wasn't in the mood for one. "It's just—you cut me short the last time I was down there. I hoped I might be able to pick up something more if I was by myself."

"Did you?"

"Yes," I said. "At least, at first. Lucien's spirit is definitely hanging around there. He tried to communicate with me, but I couldn't understand what he was saying. Something about something vile and something huge."

Calvin rubbed his chin. Although it was late in the day, I didn't notice much stubble. "Was he trying to describe the person who murdered him?"

"Possibly. His spirit was very agitated, and so I think that was making it harder for him to get his point across."

That piece of information didn't seem to sit very well. Alarm flickered in Calvin's eyes, and he asked, "Agitated how?"

I shrugged. "He was manifesting as a wind. It broke a branch off a tree and pulled the scrunchie out of my hair."

Remembering the scene, I frowned. That had been one of my favorite scrunchies.

"You could have been hurt."

"I don't think so," I said quickly. Why I felt compelled to defend Lucien, I didn't know. Most likely, I just didn't want to upset Calvin. "The branch didn't fall anywhere near me. But it doesn't matter, because you called, and that interruption was enough to break up his energy. He disappeared, and we're not any closer to figuring out who the suspect is than we were before."

His expression was still troubled, but to my relief, he didn't give me any more grief over going down to the river. Was it possible he felt a little guilty about calling at exactly the wrong time?

"You tried," he said. "And we're working the other angles."

"Like the medallion," I replied. "Any news on that?"

A pause, and I wondered if he was going to tell me for the umpteenth time that he couldn't discuss the particulars of the case with me.

It seemed he'd given that up as a lost cause, though, because he said, "We found a partial print on it, but so far that doesn't seem to be much of a lead, since it's not pinging any of our databases. Otherwise, there wasn't anything else. No DNA or something that might give us a clue to who it belonged to."

I'd expected as much—even if it had been spattered with blood during the murder, spending more than twenty-four hours underwater in the riverbed would have pretty much wiped it clean.

"That's too bad," I said.

He gave a philosophical lift of his shoulders.

"It happens. Not that I've worked many murder cases, but a lot of the time, it's two steps forward, one step back. We'll get to the bottom of it eventually."

I hoped he was right. Since he had a lot more experience in this sort of thing than I did, I'd have to take his word for it. "And Travis's car?"

Calvin shook his head. "Nothing. No mechanical failure, no signs of tampering. Chief Lewis wants to blame it on Travis driving under the influence, but he seemed sober enough. Shaken, but I didn't see any sign of him being high."

I had to agree with that assessment. True, Travis seemed pretty loopy even when he was dead sober, but his eyes weren't red or watery, and he hadn't shown any other signs of having smoked a bowl—or however he partook—before heading out that night to drive Athene to the airport.

"That's what I was worried about," I said, and Calvin lifted an eyebrow.

"That Travis wasn't smoking?"

"No, that it was a hex that made him roll the car. Dark magic like that wouldn't leave any sign behind—at least, not any sign that a regular person would be able to find."

He shot me a dubious glance. "Would you be able to find it?"

"Probably not," I admitted. "I mean, I sensed

something off about it when we were out there that night. But a strong enough practitioner wouldn't have to do something as obvious as writing a sigil on the car. They could have just set their intentions and performed a ritual from miles away."

"Well, that's comforting."

I gave an uneasy chuckle. "I know, right? But it's not as if even the people who practice that kind of dark magic are going around casting hexes right and left. That would take an enormous amount of energy…and it would attract way too much attention."

"I suppose that's a good thing, but it still leaves us without any clues we can work with." He stuck his thumbs in his belt loops and rocked back slightly on his heels, now looking almost uncomfortable. "About dinner last night—"

"Don't," I cut in, and he sent me a surprised look. "That is," I went on, realizing I'd already put my foot in it and now had no choice but to continue, "things are kind of crazy right now. We don't have to make it be anything more than dinner. My way of saying thanks for keeping me in the loop on your investigation."

His expression was now puzzled, and I wondered if I'd made a bigger hash of things than I'd thought. But he only said, "Sure. I need to get back to the station, so—"

"Right," I said, even as disappointment stabbed through me. It had been too much to hope that he'd stick around this time, especially since we'd had dinner the night before. "Thanks for bringing me my knives. I could have gone to the station to pick them up, you know."

"I know," he replied, "but I was in Globe to talk to Chief Lewis about Travis's car anyway. If anything else comes up, I'll let you know."

That was probably the most I could hope for. At least it sounded as if he planned to keep me in the loop and wasn't going to disappear forever.

I walked Calvin to the door, and we made our goodbyes. As I shut it behind him, I wondered if I'd somehow blown my opportunity with him, if we'd ever get a second chance to make a connection.

The rest of the evening felt curiously flat. I fed Archie and made myself a spinach salad topped with bits of shredded leftover chicken from my dinner with Calvin the night before, but as a meal, it was less than satisfying. It seemed as if the more times he visited my apartment, the emptier it felt when he wasn't there.

Reason told me that was a foolish way to look at the situation. We'd had a near miss, that was all.

These sorts of things didn't automatically fall into place, no matter what books and movies might want to tell you otherwise. Honestly, I should probably be glad he'd paid me as much attention as he had, considering the way Josie had described him as a man who didn't seem inclined to get involved with anyone.

Despite all those inner reassurances, I still found myself struggling with an overwhelming sense of anticlimax. Usually when I got that way, I sat down and did a few Tarot spreads, or meditated, or went for a walk to clear my head. With all the weirdness going on, though, I guessed that wandering around in downtown Globe, which would be mostly deserted by that point, probably wasn't a very good idea.

I didn't have cable, but I had plenty of entertainment at my fingertips, thanks to my Apple TV and all the streaming services I was subscribed to. Watching television was usually my last resort, but I decided that was the best thing to do with myself when I felt so jangly and not in tune with much of anything.

Resolutely ignoring the pint of rocky road ice cream in the freezer, I settled down on the couch and started flicking through the offerings. Nothing looked all that exciting, but I decided on a British baking show just because I knew I could depend on it to be relatively free of angst. I had enough of that in my personal life.

However, I only got about fifteen minutes into the first episode before my phone rang. I frowned, wondering if I should ignore it. I'd already seen Calvin that day, and I doubted he would be calling again so soon after our last meeting.

The call could be from my mother. We'd talked the day before the shop opening, and she'd promised to call again in a few days to see how everything went.

I reached for the phone and looked down at the screen. The call was coming from a number in the 818 area code, but I didn't recognize it.

My fingers hovered over the phone for a second before something compelled me to pick it up and raise it to my ear. "Hello?"

"S-Selena Marx?"

A woman's voice, very young-sounding. "This is Selena. Who's this?"

She pulled in a gasp that sounded halfway like a sob. "It—it's Violet Clarke."

Holy crap. I sat up straighter on the sofa, phone clenched against my ear. "Violet! Are you okay?"

"Y-yes. I mean, I'm okay for now. I need to talk to you."

"Where are you?"

"In Globe. I'm in the Walmart parking lot."

Her voice continued to shake, as if she was just on the verge of breaking into tears but had somehow managed to hold it together so far. I remembered how young she was, and wondered if I would have been able to maintain even that shaky a level of composure if I'd been put in the same situation when I was just nineteen.

"Do you need me to come get you?"

"N-no," she said. "Can I come to your place?"

"Sure," I replied. Reason kicked in a moment later, and I wondered if that was such a good idea. Wouldn't it be smarter to take her to see Calvin?

But I'd already said yes, and as upset as she sounded, I doubted she wanted to talk to any cops right away. Maybe later, after I'd gotten her calmed down….

"Th-thanks so much," she said. "You're in the apartment above the shop, right?"

"Yes," I said, wondering how she knew that. Then I remembered that she'd been with Lucien the night of the store opening, even if she hadn't gone with him. Probably, he'd told her all about it.

"I'll be there in a couple of minutes."

The call ended, and I sat there, staring down at the phone in my hand. Once again, I wondered if I should call Calvin. Not to have him come over and grill the kid, but just so he would know she was back in town.

Where had she gone…and why had she returned?

I reassured myself that those answers would be forthcoming soon enough. At least, I hoped they would. I told myself that I couldn't press her too hard. I'd just do my best to be supportive, and, with any luck, she'd tell me what had happened the night of Lucien's death. As to why she'd reached out to me…well, if nothing else, I was the only person in the area with any connection to Lucien, now that Athene was dead. In times of crisis, it was human nature to grasp for something that felt even halfway normal.

Should I put on a kettle in case she wanted a cup of tea?

Did she even drink tea? I could make coffee, but that didn't seem nearly as reassuring. Since she was underage, I couldn't exactly offer her a glass of wine.

Somehow, I managed to stop dithering long enough to refill the kettle and set it on the stove. Archie, who'd been curled up in the easy chair, opened an eye and shot me an annoyed look.

"Some of us are trying to sleep, you know."

"Then go sleep in your bed in the office," I said helpfully.

His lip curled, but he got up, arched his back, and then jumped down from the chair before stalking out of the room.

Probably just as well.

The buzzer sounded from downstairs a minute later, and I raced down the steps, not wanting to risk Violet losing her courage and deciding to go back from whence she came. To my relief, she was still on the back step, slim form shrouded in a black cloak with the hood pulled up to conceal her features.

As a means of disguising herself, I didn't know how effective the getup was, considering cloaks were in pretty short supply in Globe. But I only said, "Come in, Violet," then got out of the way so she could step inside. "My apartment is upstairs," I added, speaking quickly so she wouldn't get a chance to change her mind about being there. "Come on up."

She followed me up the stairwell and then into the apartment. What she thought of it, I couldn't really tell; she dropped the hood as she looked around, but her face was pale, her eyes wide and tragic.

The kettle chose that moment to begin whistling, and she startled, her slender form literally jumping an inch or two before she realized where the sound was coming from.

"Sorry about that," I said quickly, then hurried into the kitchen to shut off the gas. "I thought you might like a cup of tea. It always helps to calm me down."

"Peppermint?" she asked, sounding like a little girl inquiring if she could have another cookie.

"Absolutely," I responded in my heartiest tones. I got out a box of Traditional Medicinals peppermint tea and made some for both of us. Frankly, my nerves needed a bit of settling, too.

A mug in either hand, I went back out to the living room and set them down on the coffee table in front of the sofa. Violet took a seat, then reached for one of the mugs and held it between her hands as if she needed it to warm her chilled fingers.

She looked cold, pale and waif-like. When I'd first spotted her at Lucien's house months ago, she'd seemed almost arrogantly beautiful, like one of those absurdly young models who turned into a fierce Amazon as soon as she started marching down the catwalk. Now, though, she seemed horribly diminished, someone way out of her depth.

Well, she wasn't the only one. I still didn't know what the heck was going on, but I told myself I had ten years on her, and so I needed to act like the adult in this situation.

"Are you hurt?" I asked.

A shake of her head. "No, I'm okay." She paused, pale lips pressed together. "I mean, I'm not…but I guess I am."

I picked apart that bundle of contradictions

and determined that she meant she was physically okay. Psychologically, on the other hand....

I wished I could see her aura, but that particular gift seemed to have deserted me for the moment. Yes, I was used to it coming and going. Still, its timing seemed even crappier than usual.

"Can you tell me what happened?" I'd asked the same question of Lucien's spirit earlier that day, but I hoped this time I might actually get an intelligible answer.

Her fingers clenched more tightly around the mug she held. She lifted it and took a very small sip, wincing a little at the heat. Voice flat, she replied, "I saw Lucien get murdered, if that's what you're asking."

Dear Goddess. I rubbed my damp palms over the knees of my jeans. "I'm so sorry."

"It's...." The word trailed off, as if she honestly hadn't known what she intended to say. "I was going to say 'it's okay,' but it's really not."

At a loss, I waited, telling myself that sometimes all you could do was hold off until a person came to the right psychological moment to speak. I'd dealt with this sort of thing in my practice before, although I'd never had a client who'd been traumatized by witnessing a murder. And she was traumatized. If she'd been any paler, she would have looked as though she was ready to pass out, and a tremor went through her as she stared down at her mug of tea.

Finally, she continued. "We performed the protection ritual at the Airbnb," she said, speaking distinctly, her tone almost detached. I got the feeling that she was trying to describe Friday night's events as though they'd happened to someone else, that doing so would make it a little easier for her to tell me what exactly had transpired. "But afterward, Lucien still seemed restless. I told him we should go out to the woods and make love in the moonlight."

"That was your idea?" I asked, doing my best to rid my mind of that particular mental image.

Her lip curled, and she lifted the mug of tea and drank a slightly larger swallow. "Yeah. Does that freak you out or something?"

"No," I said calmly. "You're an adult, after all."

Those words seemed to reassure her. She sipped some more tea, then continued. "So, we went out into the woods. It was cold, but we'd brought a couple of blankets with us from the Airbnb. And actually, it was beautiful, with the sound of the river in the background and a gibbous moon overhead." A little hitch of a breath, and she blinked away the tears that came to her eyes as she recalled one of the final moments she'd shared with Lucien Dumond. "We got dressed and were folding up the blankets, getting ready to go back to the car."

She stopped there, pausing so long, I wondered if she'd decided she wasn't up to this after all and wasn't going to complete her story. But after she pulled in a ragged little breath, she resumed the tale.

"All I heard was a rustling in the leaves underfoot. Someone—something—came out of the trees and went straight for Lucien."

"Some*thing?*" I repeated. "You mean it wasn't human?" Once again, I experienced a nasty little chill down my spine. Were my earlier suspicions about a nonhuman entity being the true murderer correct?

"I don't know what it was," she said. She leaned over and set the mug of peppermint tea on the coffee table, then crossed her arms and tucked her hands under them, as if trying desperately to get warm. "It was huge—much taller than Lucien. Tall and dark."

"Like someone with dark hair and a dark complexion?"

Violet shook her head. "No…just dark. It was a shape. That's all. I couldn't see anything else." Her teeth caught on her lower lip, small and white and perfect. "I mean, until I saw the knife. It flashed in the moonlight. I saw it go into Lucien's chest, over and over."

"That's okay," I said soothingly. "You don't have to give me any more details. What happened after that?"

"Lucien sort of staggered over to the river and fell in it. He didn't move. The—the whatever it was—turned toward me. I screamed and ran." Tears began to slip from the corners of her eyes. She blinked, then reached up with one hand to wipe them away. "I know I should have stayed to check on Lucien, but I was so scared—"

Should I reach over and pat her on the arm? Probably not; she was holding herself rigid, and I had a feeling she wasn't in the mood to have anyone invade her personal space like that. "It's fine," I told her. "No one would have expected you to stay when you were being confronted by a dangerous stranger like that."

A faint nod, and she sniffled. "Maybe. Anyway, I ran to the highway. A guy gave me a ride back to Globe, and I got in my car and left."

"Why didn't you tell Athene what had happened?"

Another sniff. "She wouldn't have believed me. She hated me."

True, Athene had acted as if she didn't have much use for Violet Clarke, but "hate" was a pretty strong word. I didn't bother to rebuke her, though, reminding myself once again that the girl was barely out of high school and had traveled on her own to a strange place where she didn't know anyone, only to see her lover murdered right in front of her eyes.

Probably, I should cut her a little slack.

But while her story had answered a few questions, it left a lot open. She was sipping more of her tea, so I decided to leave the issue of Athene's feelings for Violet behind and move on to a different piece of the puzzle. "Where did you go? Chief Standingbear told me that a gas station attendant had spotted your car heading east on Highway 70."

Violet was silent for a moment. She still gripped the mug like it was the only thing grounding her in this reality. Then her thin shoulders lifted and she said, "I just needed to get away. I was worried that whatever was stalking Lucien and me would track me back to L.A., so I went in the opposite direction. I hadn't really gotten my stuff out of the car yet, so I had my bags with me. Except I didn't have a lot of cash, and I knew if I used my debit card, my parents would figure out where I had gone."

That explanation seemed logical enough. It made me a little sad, though, thinking of her parents, of how she'd taken off and hadn't told them where she was going.

How worried they must be. Or maybe not. If they were that involved in their daughter's life, wouldn't they have worked a little harder to keep her away from Lucien Dumond?

Why Violet had reached out to me, I didn't know. Maybe it really was that I was the only person in Globe she knew...and that she also knew I was safe because I'd never had any designs on Lucien.

"You really should call your parents," I said, but I kept my tone gentle, trying to let her know it was just a suggestion and not something I'd make her do in exchange for my help.

Her fingers tightened on the mug. "I know. But...can I call them in the morning? I just can't deal right now."

I knew the feeling. "Sure," I replied. "You can crash on the couch—that's all I've got, since I use the second bedroom as an office."

"Oh, that's okay," she said, expression immediately brightening. Then she added, the words rushed, as though she'd just realized that she should show some kind of gratitude for my offer, "Thanks, Selena. I really appreciate it."

"It's no problem," I told her, although I had to wonder whether it would turn out to be one.

But no—she'd crash here, and she'd call her parents in the morning, and either they'd come get her, or they'd read her the riot act and tell her she needed to get herself home immediately. Either way, it wasn't really my problem.

In the meantime, I'd get her a blanket and an extra pillow, and hope she'd have a somewhat restful night's sleep. The apartment had been recently cleansed and protected, and so I had to believe that no evil dreams would reach her.

"Do you need to get your bags out of your car?" I asked next.

At once, she shook her head. "No. I mean, I've got a travel toothbrush and toothpaste in my purse, and I can get the rest of my stuff in the morning. I don't want to go back down there in the dark."

I wanted to tell her she'd be perfectly safe, but I could sense she didn't want to hear it. After what she'd been through, she had every right to be rattled.

So I showed her where the guest bathroom was, and loaned her an old T-shirt to sleep in, and got a blanket and a pillow from the linen closet. Afterward, I escaped into my bedroom and shut the door, and did my own nighttime prep. It was only as I set my phone down on the bedside table after turning off the ringer that I paused.

Calvin really needed to know Violet was okay. Problem was, I knew if I texted him to tell him she was staying at my place, he'd be right over, and the girl needed to rest. He could talk to her in the morning.

I decided to compromise. I picked up the phone and sent a brief text: *Violet is safe.*

That should be enough. We could sort out the details in the morning.

I put the phone back down and lay back against the pillows. From outside my closed door, I heard the faint whisper of water running, and then the even lighter pad of Violet's bare feet as she headed back to the living room. Silence after that, and I closed my eyes and released a breath.

But even though I knew I should be trying to sleep, my thoughts couldn't seem to calm themselves enough for me to reach that state. Something kept picking at the edges of my mind, telling me I'd missed something big.

What, though?

I rolled over on my side and released a breath. The scene down at the river replayed in my mind's eye. The angry, restless wind which was all that remained of Lucien Dumond. The howl of that disembodied voice.

Vile....

Huge....

My eyes flared open, and I shifted onto my back again as I stared up at the ceiling.

What if Lucien hadn't been saying "vile," but had been trying to utter the word "Violet"?

And "Huge"?

Lucien's younger brother was named Eugene.

He'd never been even on the periphery of GLANG, but....

Oh, dear Goddess.

I sat up in bed, alarm shrilling through me. But even as I was reaching down to push back the bedcovers, the door to my bedroom flew open.

Standing in the doorway were two figures, one short and slender, the other tall and bulky. The light in the hallway made a halo of her blonde hair, although I doubted she was an angel.

The taller figure moved into my bedroom.

"Hello, Selena," said Eugene Dershowitz.

16

Family Ties

We sat in the living room, Eugene and Violet pressed up against each other in a way that told me everything I needed to know about their relationship, while I occupied the easy chair.

Not that there was anything particularly easy about my state of mind right then, although I found myself incongruously relieved that I'd taken to sleeping in loose tank tops and yoga pants after I started cohabiting with Archie, rather than going to bed in a pair of panties and nothing else the way I used to back in L.A.

"You did it," I said, my tone flat.

"Did your psychic powers tell you that?" Eugene asked with a sneer. He resembled his brother a good deal, although he had a head of thick black hair, very unlike his brother's shaved pate. Somehow, he managed to be even less attractive than Lucien.

"I don't need psychic powers to put two and two together," I said coolly.

Violet sent me an evil little smile. "Eugene has always been really good at hiding his powers. Lucien had no idea that his little brother was actually stronger than he was."

"And so you decided to murder him so you could inherit everything?"

Eugene shrugged. "'Murder' is a very strong word. Let's just say that I thought it was a good time for my big brother to move on from this life to his next turn on the wheel of existence."

"But you still wanted the money."

Violet's expression turned condescending. "Well, duh. Except the problem was that Lucien had made Athene his heir, and Eugene would only inherit his money if she was dead, too. So we had to take care of that problem as well. Luckily, the both of them being here in Globe and away from all the protection spells they'd cast on their homes back in L.A. was all the opening we needed."

While that revelation made some sense, I couldn't ignore one inconsistency in the narrative. "But you helped him cast a protection spell on Friday night," I pointed out. "Athene told me about it."

"Using sex magic," Violet replied before adding with a smirk, "I faked it."

Ah. Well, if she'd pretended to have an orgasm, then the spell wouldn't have been solid... and it would have left both Lucien and Athene open to magical attack.

"And where do I come in?" I asked, doing my best to sound calm. I had to guess they didn't mind telling me the truth because they planned to get rid of my troublesome self as soon as I'd done whatever it was that they needed from me.

The couple exchanged a glance. Looking at them, I had to wonder how they'd managed to conceal their relationship from Lucien. The man had his faults, but no one could have accused him of being imperceptive.

On the other hand, he also had an ego the size of the *Titanic*. Most likely, he hadn't seen the signs because he couldn't allow himself to believe that anyone would prefer his far less talented and charismatic brother over himself.

Except Eugene had turned out to be just as powerful after all.

He frowned. His eyebrows were as sparse as his brother's, an odd contrast to his thick hair. Maybe he'd had a little help in that department, either via some kind of enchantment...or a life-time membership in Hair Club for Men.

"Lucien hid his will," he said. "I've looked

everywhere, and I can't find it. He must have put some kind of concealment spell on it."

"What makes you think I would know where it is?" I asked. "Lucien never mentioned a will to me."

"Maybe not, but you can talk to him, right?"

I stared at Eugene in consternation. How could he know that?

Looking smug, he went on, "Yes, I was down by the river when you had your little *tête-à-tête* with my dearly departed brother. Poor guy was having a hard time getting the words out, wasn't he? But you still could hear him."

Too bad I didn't understand what he was trying to tell me until it was too late, I thought. If I'd only put the pieces together even ten minutes earlier....

But that couldn't be helped now. I had to pretend to go along with their wishes until I could come up with a way to extricate myself from the stickiest situation I'd ever found myself in.

"So...you want me to talk to Lucien so he'll reveal the location of his will?" I asked.

"Exactly. Then we'll go back to Los Angeles, and you can go on with...well, whatever it is you're doing in this useless little town."

I bristled with indignation on Globe's behalf, although I knew I had far bigger things to worry about than Eugene Dershowitz impugning my adopted hometown's reputation. Maybe I wasn't exactly familiar with how cold-blooded killers operated, but every instinct was telling me that he was lying, and that he and Violet had absolutely no intention of allowing me to keep breathing after I'd given them what they wanted.

And actually, I didn't need instincts, not when I could see the flicker of murderous blood-red points all through Eugene's murky aura. Violet's wasn't much better, although the odd little yellow and orange surges through her aura seemed to indicate more amusement at watching me squirm than simple bloodlust. Nice of that particular gift to make an appearance now, although it would have been a lot more helpful when Violet first appeared at my apartment.

"So, we're going back down to the river?" I asked. That notion didn't sit very well with me, mostly because Eugene had already proved that he thought it was a great place for a quiet little murder.

"No," he replied, and relief flooded through me. "I don't want to give anyone a chance to interfere. You've got a crystal ball, right?"

"Yes."

"We'll use that to contact him. Go get it."

I wanted to tell him he couldn't order me around like one of his brother's GLANG lackeys, but I realized I didn't have much say in the matter, thanks to my current situation. Without replying, I got up from the easy chair and headed into the office. Eugene followed, probably to make sure I wouldn't try to call for help.

The image of my phone lying on the table next to my bed passed through my mind, but I knew there was no way I could slip into the bedroom to grab it, not with Eugene like an evil shadow on my trail. I turned on the light in the office, murmuring a silent apology to Archie for barging in like this, although I didn't see him in his bed. Well, he also liked to curl up on the rug in front of the stacking washer/dryer in the laundry room, so maybe that was where he'd headed.

I hoped so. This night might be my last on earth, but I didn't want poor Archie sucked into the whole sorry mess. He already had enough to worry about.

Silently, I went over to the altar and lifted the crystal ball and its stand from the table. I hated letting Eugene see that sacred space—altars tended to be private, although I hadn't had a problem with Calvin getting a look—but I doubted he would have heeded any requests to stay in the hallway.

"Back to the living room," Eugene commanded, and I stalked past him, head held high. Maybe he planned to kill me in some gruesome magical way after I'd given him what he wanted—ritual sacrifice or something—but I wasn't about to let him see how shaken I was.

When we got back, I noticed that Violet had changed out of the oversized T-shirt I'd lent her and back into the black dress she'd been wearing when she first turned up on my doorstep. If only the universe had sent me a sign that she was up to no good—a tingle down my back, or even something as simple as the call dropping so she couldn't ask to come over.

Not that she would have given up so easily.

I set the crystal ball down on the coffee table. Eugene didn't sit, but remained hovering near my elbow. I was just about to tell him to back off, that I couldn't focus with someone so obviously invading my space, but then a flicker of an idea passed through my mind.

No way of knowing whether it would work, but I had to try.

I closed my eyes and placed my hands on the crystal ball, doing my best to put on a good show. Actually, the last thing I wanted to do was contact Lucien's ghost. My crystal ball had now resonated with my Grandma Ellen's spirit for so many years, I honestly didn't even know whether it would allow me to communicate with anyone else. Even if it did, though, I didn't want Lucien's presence entering it, fouling it. My cleansing rituals were usually very effective, but I somehow doubted they were up to the task of scrubbing Lucien Dumond out of the crystal's intricate lattices.

And you know, that crystal ball had been very expensive. I really didn't want to be forced into buying a new one.

If I survived all of this, of course.

"*Lucien*," I breathed, trying my best to sound sepulchral. I always spoke to Grandma Ellen in normal tones, but obviously, Eugene didn't know that. And even though I couldn't see her with my eyes shut, I sensed that Violet had moved toward the edge of the sofa, was perched there as she watched the scene with avid eyes.

Well, obviously, she'd be eager. Who knew how many millions of dollars were on the line?

What I heard next wasn't Lucien's reedy baritone, though, but my grandmother's no-nonsense tones.

Get him, sweetie!

I didn't even stop to think. My hands tightened on the crystal ball, and I lifted it from its stand and swung it right at Eugene's head.

The ten-pound crystal connected with his skull with a *crack* that made me wince. He let out an *oof!* and staggered backward before tripping over the edge of the rug. Balance lost, he went down like a ton of bricks, head hitting the hardwood floor with another loud *crack*.

"You bit—" Violet began, lunging up from the couch so she could grab my arm.

Before she could even finish the epithet, a blur of gray fur landed on her head, hissing and biting and scratching. She let out an unholy howl, hands flashing up to protect her face. Blinded, she tripped over the coffee table and went flying, landing with a clatter on the fireplace tools I had sitting by the hearth, right before her head smacked into the glass doors that protected the fireplace. Her body went slack, and then the front door to the apartment flew open.

Calvin's voice echoed down the hall. "Selena! Are you okay?"

Hands shaking, I put the crystal ball back in its stand. I glanced over at the cat, who was now sitting on the sofa, looking very satisfied with himself. "Thanks for the assist, Archie."

"You're welcome," he said primly. "I hope you'll remember this the next time you're buying me treats."

About all I could do was shake my head. Then I raised my voice and said, "I'm okay, Calvin. But I think we've got a bit of a clean-up on Aisle Four."

He hurried into the room, then stopped short at the sight of Eugene passed out on the floor, and an equally unconscious but also bloody Violet

Clarke with her head halfway into the fireplace. "What the hell happened?"

"Our perps got greedy," I said.

"Violet was the killer?" he asked, expression disbelieving.

"Accomplice," I told him. "The actual murderer is Eugene here. Eugene Dershowitz," I added. "Lucien's little brother."

"Damn." Calvin shook his head, then sent a worried glance down at Eugene, who'd just let out a moan and began to stir. "And here I left my handcuffs at home. Do you have any zip ties, bungee cords…a spare extension cord?"

"I have some extension cords," I said. "Let me go grab them."

Luckily, I'd stored them in the catch-all drawer in the kitchen, so it didn't take me any time at all to go grab the cords—left over from my move, when I wasn't sure how many I would need—and hand them over to Calvin. With grim efficiency, he bound Eugene's hands, then went over and extricated Violet from the fireplace as gently as he could. She groaned, her face a mass of bloody little cuts. They'd heal eventually…but I had a feeling they'd leave quite a few scars.

Karma could be an efficient but ruthless teacher.

Then Calvin was on the phone, calling for an ambulance, calling Globe P.D. so they could get a couple of deputies over to the apartment. I was glad of the way he'd taken over the situation, the way he knew exactly what to do. My hands were shaking so badly, I didn't know whether I could have even dialed 9-1-1.

From inside the crystal ball, my grandmother winked at me. *Good work, my girl,* came her voice, sounding in only my ears.

Thank the Goddess that none of the cops who showed up could hear it.

I wandered down the riverbank to the hidden little beach where Lucien Dumond had died at his brother's hands. I wanted to tell him myself what had happened, that justice had been served and there was no longer any need for him to linger on this plane.

Quite possibly, he already knew, but I still felt like I had a duty to give him some closure.

Or maybe the only closure I needed was for myself.

Eugene Dershowitz and Violet Clarke were both in jail, awaiting a court date. According to Calvin, both their families had descended on Chief Lewis, demanding that they be released on bail. But Lewis, hard-ass that he was, said the judge had determined they were both flight risks, and so they would remain locked up until they had their day in court.

And since they had an eyewitness who had heard both of them confess to the murders of Lucien Dumond and Athene Kappas, everyone figured it was going to be a very short trial. It also sounded as if Violet was angling for a reduced sentence in return for her cooperation—her lawyer was leaning heavily on her youth and the fact that she didn't have any priors—but so far, it didn't seem as if the local D.A. was inclined to go along with that plan.

"Lucien?" I called out, my voice questioning. I didn't want to be too forceful; if he'd already moved on, then I didn't want to do anything that would draw him back to this place.

But there he was, shimmering into existence a few feet away from where I stood. His ghost looked hearty enough, with color in his cheeks and even a faint smile on his lips.

"Selena," he said.

"I hope I didn't disturb you."

He shook his head. "No, I was actually getting ready to move on, but I sensed you wanted to talk to me."

"I guess I just wanted to know you would be okay." When he was alive, I had definitely not been one of Lucien's fan club, but I still hated the thought of him being trapped in this place forever.

He'd definitely been a schmuck, but I still didn't believe he deserved to be murdered by his brother, nor plotted against by a woman he'd thought cared for him.

Or maybe he had. The universe had dispensed its own justice in the end.

"I am okay." He paused there, still smiling. "Or at least, I'm starting to see the light at the end of the tunnel. At any rate, I think I learned a few things from this life."

I had to hope I would be that philosophical when the time came. Being dead did seem to give a person new perspective.

"Well, that's good," I replied. "And I think Eugene and Violet will be going to prison for a long time."

Those words only elicited a small shrug. "I'm not sure that will allow them to learn the things they need to learn, but that's their own path to take."

I sort of hated to ask, but since this might very well be my only chance to get the facts straight from the horse's mouth—so to speak—I said, "Where's the knife? Calvin didn't find it in Eugene's possessions."

"In there." Lucien pointed toward the glinting waters of the San Ramon River. "He threw it downstream after he wiped it clean." A pause, and then he added, "It was sort of strange to stand here and watch him do that, even as I realized I was dead."

"Yes, I suppose it would be," I said carefully. He didn't look overly troubled by the recollection, but still. "And Violet's medallion?"

Not even a blink. "Just as Eugene attacked—and she stood and watched—I reached out and pulled it off her neck. She didn't deserve to be wearing it, the little traitor."

No, I supposed not. But at least his reply cleared up that part of the mystery.

Lucien went on, "Of course, the irony of the whole situation is that the joke would have been on them even if they'd been successful in their scheme."

I tilted my head at him. "I don't understand."

His mouth twitched slightly. "Before I left to see you here in Globe, I had my will changed. I'd begun to sense that Eugene possibly wasn't the best person to have as my fall-back heir, for reasons that are now obvious. My lawyer rewrote the will to name you and Athene as my two beneficiaries."

For a second or two, all I could do was stand there and stare at him. He smiled back at me like a tattooed Buddha. "*W-what?*" I finally managed. "And Athene was on board with this?"

"Well, she thought I was slightly mad, but she also said it was my money to do with as I pleased."

Lucien stopped there and flicked an imaginary piece of dust off the sleeve of his black shirt. "Of course, since she's now gone as well, it will all go to you."

I thought I needed to sit down. There was an old tree stump not too far from where I stood, so I made my way over to it and shakily lowered myself to a sitting position. "What am I supposed to do with all that money?"

"Whatever you want. Keep it, give it away— it's all the same to me." He sent me another of those enigmatic smiles. "I think we would've made a good team, if you'd given me a chance."

I had my own doubts on that topic, but I didn't feel like arguing with a ghost. If he wanted to drift off to his next spin on the wheel thinking that we would have made a love connection in this life, so be it.

"I'll figure something out," I said.

"I know you will—and you'll be hearing from my lawyer soon. Goodbye, Selena."

He faded away, leaving me sitting there alone on my tree stump.

Well, then. Apparently, I was going to be a millionaire.

I didn't quite know what to think about that.

Calvin came up the stairs just as Brett Woodrow was leaving. The two men nodded at each other, and Calvin gave me an inquiring look as I shut the door behind him.

"He was giving me an estimate on replacing the fireplace doors," I explained.

"Right." He glanced over at the fireplace in question, which didn't look too bad, since Brett had removed the remnants of the shattered glass, leaving it bare-faced for now. Because we were heading into late spring and then summer, I wasn't too worried about not being able to use it. The replacements would be installed long before the weather got cold enough for me to have a fire.

"How was your trip to California?" Calvin asked then. He looked oddly diffident, as if he wasn't sure how he was supposed to act around me.

But then, he wasn't the only one who'd been doing that same tiptoeing. I think everyone assumed that since I'd inherited vast sums of money from Lucien—and because he was out of the picture permanently—I'd just naturally want to move back to California.

However, I'd known almost as soon as I stepped off the plane at Bob Hope Airport in Burbank that I'd made the right decision in moving to Globe. I still had a lot to learn about small-town living, but I could tell it was the right fit for me. I'd met with Lucien's lawyer and a financial consultant and the real estate agent who was handling the sale of his house, stopped in to see my mother and her husband, and then gotten right back on the plane. The whole trip had taken less than the space of a day, but I still felt as though I'd been away from Arizona for too long.

"It was fine," I said. "A lot of loose ends to tie up, but things are progressing. I'll get it figured out eventually."

I'd decided not too long after my meeting with Lucien's ghost in the woods that I didn't want to keep most of his money. Enough so my already plump cushion would be padded that much more, but I'd already started dispensing large chunks of the rest of it to my favorite charities. Quite a bit more would go to local causes, like Josie's theater guild and the high school, which was in desperate need of a new auditorium.

Things like that. I had no idea whether Lucien would be amused by my altruism, or irritated that the empire he'd built during his lifetime was being broken up so easily.

Quite possibly, a little of both.

Calvin's expression was unreadable. "What does it feel like to be a millionaire?"

"The same, I guess," I told him. "I don't think it's really sunk in yet. Probably a good thing."

"Hmm."

He'd sent me a text asking if he could come over, and of course I'd said yes. Now, though, I had to wonder exactly what it was he'd had in mind.

"I was thinking," he said, then paused.

"'Thinking'?" I prompted him.

A flash of that knee-weakening grin. "You made dinner for me the other day. It just seems like I should return the favor."

Was he suggesting what I thought he was suggesting?

"Problem is," he continued. "I'm not much of a cook. So, I was kind of hoping you'd let me buy you dinner."

I placed my hands on my hips. "Calvin Stand-ingbear, are you asking me out on a date?"

He appeared to consider, then nodded. "I think I am. If that's all right with you."

Smiling, I said, "Oh, I think that's *very* all right."

"Good," he said. "Tomorrow at seven?"

"Sure," I replied, feeling somewhat dazed.

He didn't say anything else, only nodded and then headed off toward the door.

As soon as he was gone, Archie stuck his head around the corner. "Are you going out to dinner with that man?"

"I guess I am."

The cat frowned before asking sourly, "This is going to lead to sex, isn't it?"

I stared at the door Calvin had disappeared through just a moment earlier.

"I sure hope so," I said.

Hedgewitch for Hire will continue in *Social Medium,* releasing on March 31, 2021. Be sure to sign up for Christine Pope's mailing list so you don't miss a thing!

Author's Note

Globe is a real town, located in Gila County in the south-central part of Arizona. Like Jerome, it's a former mining town, although with its own particular flavor. For the purposes of this series, however, I've changed some of the town's elements and embellished others. The San Ramon Apache, while based on the San Carlos Apache in the region, are my own invention, for reasons that will become obvious as the series goes on. Most of the local points of interest are also invented, although some of them are based on real-world versions.

I hope you've enjoyed this visit to Globe, and will return for Selena and Calvin's continuing adventures.

Christine Pope
New Mexico, December 2020

Also by Christine Pope

HEDGEWITCH FOR HIRE

(Mystery/Paranormal romance)

Grave Mistake

Social Medium (March 2021)

Household Demons (July 2021)

Perpetual Potion (October 2021)

———

THE WITCHES OF WHEELER PARK

(Paranormal romance)

Storm Born

Thunder Road

Winds of Change

Mind Games

A Wheeler Park Christmas

Blood Ties (February 2021)

Healing Hands (May 2021)

Wishful Thinking (September 2021)

PROJECT DEMON HUNTERS*

(Paranormal Romance)

Unquiet Souls

Unbound Spirits

Unholy Ground

Unseen Voices

Unmarked Graves

Unbroken Vows

———

THE DEVIL YOU KNOW*

(Paranormal Romance)

Sympathy for the Devil

Charmed, I'm Sure

A Wing and a Prayer

———

THE WITCHES OF CANYON ROAD*

(Paranormal Romance)

Hidden Gifts

Darker Paths

Mysterious Ways

A Canyon Road Christmas

Demon Born

An Ill Wind

Higher Ground

Haunted Hearts

THE WITCHES OF CLEOPATRA HILL*

(Paranormal Romance)

Darkangel

Darknight

Darkmoon

Sympathetic Magic

Protector

Spellbound

A Cleopatra Hill Christmas

Impractical Magic

Strange Magic

The Arrangement

Defender

Bad Blood

Deep Magic

Darktide

THE SEDONA FILES*

(Paranormal Romance)

Bad Vibrations

Desert Hearts

Angel Fire

Star Crossed

Falling Angels

Enemy Mine

———

TALES OF THE LATTER KINGDOMS*

(Fantasy Romance)

All Fall Down

Dragon Rose

Binding Spell

Ashes of Roses

One Thousand Nights

Threads of Gold

The Wolf of Harrow Hall

Moon Dance

The Song of the Thrush

———

THE GAIAN CONSORTIUM SERIES*

(Science Fiction Romance)

Beast (free prequel novella)

Blood Will Tell

Breath of Life

The Gaia Gambit

The Mandala Maneuver

The Titan Trap

The Zhore Deception

The Refugee Ruse

STANDALONE TITLES

Hearts on Fire

Taking Dictation

Golden Heart

Night Music: A Modern Reimagining of The Phantom of the Opera

Ghost Dance: A Sequel to Gaston Leroux's The Phantom of the Opera

Flight Before Christmas

* Indicates a completed series

About the Author

USA Today bestselling author Christine Pope has been writing stories ever since she commandeered her family's Smith-Corona typewriter back in grade school. Her work includes paranormal romance, fantasy romance, and science fiction/space opera romance. She makes her home in New Mexico.

Christine Pope on the Web:
www.christinepope.com

 facebook.com/ChristinePopeAuthor

 twitter.com/ChristineJPope

 pinterest.com/ChristineJPope

www.ingramcontent.com/pod-product-compliance
Lightning Source LLC
Chambersburg PA
CBHW052021240626
47153CB00006B/1895